The
Curse Girl

∂

KATE AVERY ELLISON

THE CURSE GIRL

© 2011 by Kate Avery Ellison

All rights reserved.

ISBN-13: 978-1461197942

ISBN-10: 1461197945

Printed in the United States of America

For Nikki

The
Curse Girl

ONE

MY FATHER DROVE ME me through the woods in his truck, the wheels shuddering over the dirt road while the air hummed with all the unspoken words between us. The tears wriggled down his wrinkled cheeks only to get lost in his beard. The mark on his wrist burned at the edge of my peripheral vision, as if it were glowing.

I sat silent and immobile, a statue, a paper doll, a frozen thing of stone.

When we reached the gate I drew one shuddering breath and let it out, and my father put his hand on my shoulder. His fingers dug into my skin.

"He promised he wouldn't hurt you, Bee. He *promised.*"

I shifted. His hand fell limply on the seat between us. He didn't try to touch me again.

Dad turned off the engine and we sat wrapped in the silence. I heard him swallow hard. I slid my fingers up and down the strap of my backpack. My mouth tasted like dust. The car smelled like old leather and fresh terror.

Nobody knew if the legends were lies, myth, or truth. But they all talked about the Beast that lived in the house.

Some said he ate human children, some said he turned into a vicious creature in the night, some said he looked like a demon, with flames for eyes.

A trickle of sweat slipped down my spine.

"You don't—" My father started to say, but he hesitated. Maybe he'd been hoping I would cut him off, but I didn't. I just sat, holding my backpack, feeling the crush of responsibility slip over my shoulders and twine around my neck like a noose.

Through the gate I could see the house, watching us with windows like dead eyes. Trees pressed close to the bone-white walls like huddled hags with flowing green hair, and everything was covered with a mist of grayish moss. I'd heard the stories my whole life—we all had—but I'd never been close enough to see the cracks in the windowsills, the dead vines clinging to the roof.

Magic hung in the air like the lingering traces of a memory. I could almost taste it. Voices whispered faintly in the wind, or was that just the trees? The knot in my stomach stirred in response.

My father tried again, and this time he got the whole sentence out. "You don't have to do this."

Of course I did. Of course I must.

I wasn't doing this for him. I was doing it because I had no choice. With the mark on his wrist, he was a dead man.

Our whole family was doomed. He knew it and I knew it, and he was playing a game of lame pretend because he wanted to sooth his own guilt. Because he wanted to be able to look back at this moment every time it crossed his mind in the future and feel that he had offered me a way out. That he'd been willing to rescue me, but I'd refused.

Instead of responding, I opened the door and climbed out. The gravel crunched under my shoes as I stepped to the ground. I shouldered my backpack and took a deep breath.

The gate squeaked beneath my hand. I crossed the lawn and climbed the steps to the house, feeling the stone shudder beneath my shoes like the house lived and breathed. The door didn't open on its own, which I had half-expected, but when I put my hand on the knob I could feel the energy humming inside it like a heartbeat.

My father waited at the car. I looked over my shoulder and saw him standing with one hand on the door, his shoulders pulled tight like a slingshot.

All I had to do was step inside. One step inside and the mark would disappear. And I could run home. I could outsmart this house. Couldn't I? I sucked in a deep breath and rolled my shoulders.

Maybe I believed that. Maybe I didn't. Why else had I brought a backpack full of clothes, toiletries?

"Bee," my father called out, and his voice cracked. I paused, waiting for more. Maybe he really was sorry. Maybe he really didn't want me to do this . . .

"Bee, I just wanted to tell you how thankful your stepmother and I —"

My throat tightened. He wasn't going to stop me, was he? I shook my head, and he rubbed a hand over his face and fell silent.

When he'd come home two weeks ago at three in the morning, the sleeve of his work uniform torn, his lip bleeding, and his eyes full of fear, my stepmother had cried. Really cried — wrenching sobs that made her double over and clutch at her sides. She almost looked as if she were laughing. I'd looked at him, and I could smell the magic on him. I'd known exactly where he'd been.

And there was a tiny part of me that knew then too that I'd be the one who would pay the price for his foolishness.

All I had to do now was step across the threshold. Then the mark on his wrist would vanish, and he would be free. Everything would be okay. That was all we'd promised, right?

I pushed open the door and stepped into the house. I held my breath.

Across the lawn, my father made a sound like a sob.

Was that it? Was the mark gone?

"Daddy?" I choked out, not daring to move. "Is it —?"

"It's gone, honey!"

I started to turn, but I wasn't fast enough. The door snapped shut like the jaws of a hungry animal.

I grabbed the handle and twisted, throwing my shoulder against the heavy wood. I shrieked, wrenching the handle harder.

It was locked.

I clawed at the wood with my fingernails until they bled. I pounded with my fists.

The door didn't budge. It was strong as stone.

Through the slip of glass, I saw the headlights of my father's car flick on, and the engine revved.

He was leaving me.

I slid to the floor. My sneakers squeaked against the shiny marble, my fingers slipped down the polished mahogany of the door. I didn't want to look behind me into the mouth of the house, into the darkness that was going to be my home. Or my tomb. I didn't want to think of how my father would go home and my absence would be like a ripple in the house, felt for a moment and then gone from their minds. I didn't want to think about who would miss me at school. Violet. Livia. Drew.

Drew.

Grief stuck like cement behind my eyes. I wanted to cry, but I had no tears. I never had tears. My eyes burned and my throat squeezed shut, making it hard to breathe. I crouched on the floor and put my hand over my mouth and thought of Drew's hair, his eyes, his smile.

I might never see any of those things ever again.

Terror — real terror — charged through me like a

storm. It pulsed through my body, pushing at my skin, wanting to get out. Like my own soul was fighting to be free of me, like my own self couldn't stand to be trapped here at this moment. It was a surge of blinding intensity, like lightning. Then I fell, panting, my hands braced on the cool floor.

"Stop it," I said aloud. "Stop this."

I didn't have to stay here. The mark was gone and we were free and I could go home — if I could just find a way out. The idea, planted in my fear-frozen mind, cracked my terror like spring warmth.

Escape.

After all, I wasn't dead.

"Yet," I muttered, and the echo of my voice, soft and velvet, whispered back to me in the stillness. I closed my eyes tight, counted to five, and opened them. And I looked at the place that was going to be my prison.

The foyer stretched up like a bell tower. A shattered chandelier lay three feet away, crystal droplets spread like frozen tears across the marble. Light slanted into the hall through arching windows, illuminating the rest of the room and striping the broken furniture and torn books with golden sunlight. In the middle of the room, papers and quills lay scattered around on the floor. It was as if a great monster had gone into a rage and shredded the room, and then fallen into a peaceful slumber after exhausting himself.

Behind me lurked a gloomy hallway, lined with doors.

I was stuck in this house. My friends couldn't help me. Drew couldn't help me. My father wouldn't help me.

A sigh slipped through my lips as I stood to my feet.

I was alone.

Alone in the house of the Beast.

TWO

I NEEDED TO find a way out. A window, maybe? The only light in the foyer came from the glass panel in the door and a few portals high in the vaulted ceiling. My gaze slid to the doors lining the hallway.

I'd have to go through one of them.

For a second I wondered if I could just stay here, clinging to the front door praying my father would come back with an axe to save me. But I knew that was stupid.

He wasn't coming back. I knew that deep in my bones.

Gathering a lungful of air, I rolled my shoulders and bounced in place, loosening my muscles in case I needed to run. I stepped towards the first door.

A blast of musty air fanned my face as I stared into utter darkness. A shudder crawled down my spine, and I slammed the door, my heart thudding.

I moved to the second door, but it led to blackness too. Were there no windows in this house? I'd seen them outside. They should be here somewhere.

I tried every door, and every door opened to darkness. Darkness it would be, then. Spotting a candle in a bracket on the wall, I stood on my tiptoes to grab it. I'd need light.

As soon as I'd wrapped my fingers around the waxy stick, the wick ignited in flame. I screamed and dropped it, and the fire went out. The candle rolled away, and I stumbled back, shaking.

Get a grip, Bee. I bent and snatched it up grimly. The flame flared up again as soon as my fingers closed around it. I stepped forward into the first door I'd opened.

The candle illuminated a patch of room around me. A draft from overhead swirled around my shoulders, making the flame flicker and dance. I cupped my hand around the bit of fire and walked faster, scanning the walls for windows or doors that might lead outside. I saw only dusty chairs and cobwebbed ottomans.

Memories swirled over me as I walked. Memories of my grandmother, whispering tales to me in the dark about an old house under a spell. About a monster held captive by the words of a witch. I remembered being six years old and sitting in the backyard sandbox while Sarah Albright, my next door neighbor, told me with wide eyes about how the cursed beast who lived in the house in the woods ate little children for breakfast. She swore her brother had almost been eaten and escaped at the last moment. I'd slept with a nightlight on for weeks after that.

This house was the monster in the closet the town only whispered of, and now I was swallowed inside it.

I crept on like an explorer in a cave. I passed through another door, and the walls expanded. My footsteps reverberated in the blackness, and I knew I was someplace huge. A ballroom? Maybe it was the air flow, or the change in smell, or the way my footsteps echoed. Once air brushed over my skin as though someone had moved past me, and I whirled, my heart beating wildly and panic clawing at my throat.

"Hello?" My voice fluttered like a lost bird in the darkness.

A figure stood behind me, clutching a light, their movements mimicking my own. My heart stuttered before I realized it was my reflection in a mirror. Cracks in the glass scattered the candlelight, making ribbons of light dance over my face and hands. I tipped my head back and stared up, but I couldn't see how far it went.

I moved forward again, coming to another door. I turned the knob and stepped inside. My candle cast light over a table and a massive cylindrical shape covered with a silk cloth. I reached up to touch it, curious, and the cloth fell away beneath my fingertips.

My mouth dropped open.

A massive hourglass sat on the table, glittering in the firelight. Inside the glass a steady stream of sand was pouring down, glittering faintly as if the grains were phosphorescent.

Most of the sand had already slipped through the center and piled in the bottom part of the timepiece. I could hear the rasp of the sand as it trickled down. I stretched out my fingers to touch it. For some reason, it filled me with fear.

The voice spoke from behind me. "Who's there?"

Terror shot through me like lightning, and I jerked around, almost dropping the candle. Someone was in the room with me. "Hello?" I gasped the word out as I stumbled away from the table.

Wind slipped over my arms. The flame of my candle shivered.

"Who are you? What are you doing in here?" The voice was just a whisper, but it was laced with anger.

Fear slithered down my spine. I took a step back.

"My name is Beauty."

I don't know why I used my full name instead of Bee. The word had leaped from my tongue, almost involuntarily.

He moved slowly — I couldn't see him. I heard the scrape of his feet against the ground. "What are you doing in here? You're supposed to be waiting in your room until you are called, Curse Girl."

Curse Girl? "I . . . I'm sorry."

"You shouldn't be here. This room is off limits."

I didn't know what to say. My shoulders shook. My hands grew slick. I held the candle tighter so I wouldn't drop it and be plunged into complete blindness.

"Who are you?" But I knew. I knew exactly who was snarling at me, smothered in blackness.

The Beast himself.

He moved forward so swiftly I didn't see his face. He put his hand over the candle. The light went out in a puff of smoke. I stumbled back against the mirror and he braced his hands on either side of my head.

"I'm the Beast," he growled. He was mocking me. "I'm sure you've heard terrible things about me. And now you're in my part of the house. Get out."

"Please," I said. Thoughts ran through my head — my stepsisters, my best friend Violet, Drew — I was thinking, *please please please don't kill me. I love them. I need to live.*

I realized I had whispered the words aloud.

His breath brushed my lips. "What have you been told? That I'll lock you in a dungeon? That I'll eat you? Are you scared?"

Yes, yes, and yes. But I shook my head, my hair brushing his hands. "You promised my father you wouldn't hurt me. He felt the magic in your words! You gave him a sacred promise. You can't hurt me."

My voice dropped to a whisper at the end, and it shook despite what I'd just said.

I was still terrified.

He drew away. "You don't understand. I'm not a monster. Now go back to your room and wait to be called."

And he was gone. His words were still ringing in my head.

I'm not a monster.

THREE

I WAS LEFT trembling alone in the dark. The brush with the Beast had reduced my legs to jelly, and my fingers to spaghetti noodles. I stumbled for the door, and this time when I opened it light poured over me. I stumbled into a hallway lit by blazing chandeliers. I didn't understand—hadn't this room been a dark ballroom? I'd passed through it only moments earlier. But I didn't have time to think.

A woman was standing to my left as if she'd been waiting for me all along. She flinched at my startled gasp. But I couldn't help myself.

Her white dress hung in tatters and her hair was coiled on her head in a thick, outdated bun. But it was her skin that made me gasp. Roses and scrolls against blue background covered her face, her arms, her hands. She matched the wallpaper behind her as if she'd stepped through the plaster.

My head spun the way it had when I'd ridden my first roller coaster at age twelve as I looked at her. I put out a hand to brace myself against the door.

"Welcome," she said, twisting her hands together and dropping a short curtsey. "You are the Curse Girl? Aren't you pretty! Please come with me. I'm going to take you to your room."

"I'm Beauty Hendricks," I managed, uncertain about the term *Curse Girl*. This was the second time someone had called me that. I didn't know what they meant by it.

"Yes, Beauty. We've been expecting you," she said, and there was something about the way she pronounced the word *we* that made a shiver run down my back. "I am Housekeeper."

I didn't have time to think about the odd way she said that, like her name was Housekeeper, because she started walking, and I had no choice but to follow or be left alone in the hall. And at the moment, I wanted to be with anyone but that beast in the darkness.

Maybe she would take me to a room with a window.

I followed her.

Housekeeper went to the first door in the long hallway behind us and turned the brass knob.

"Come," she said, giving me a wane, but warm, smile. "Don't mind the house."

We stepped through the doorway and into another hallway, this one carpeted with a blood-red runner and lined with statues. They grimaced at me with contorted expressions—gleeful scowls and ruinous smiles.

"Ah, the Hall of Regret," Housekeeper said, her forehead wrinkling. She looked as if she'd anticipated something else. "Well, then. This way, please."

I was still shaking. I could still feel his breath grazing my lips, his hands so close on either side of my face. Or had they been claws?

"You look so frightened, dear. Don't be alarmed. This old house has a few tricks in it, but you'll get used to them. And the Master . . ." Housekeeper trailed off as she opened the door at the end of the hall and peered inside. "This is the conservatory," she said, more to herself than to me, and she sounded irritated.

We stepped inside. Fading sunlight poured through the glass walls and glinted on broken glass and rusted lawn furniture. Dead plants covered the broken tile floor and sagged against the walls. A shard of glass crunched beneath my shoe.

My heart skipped a beat as I saw the outdoors, just beyond my reach. I quickly took stock of the room. I'd need to be able to find it again.

We kept walking through endless rooms, which I did my best to memorize so I could remember how to get back to the conservatory, which so far looked like my best bet for escape. Housekeeper took me through almost half a dozen more interior rooms — studies, parlors, a giant library with a painted ceiling, even a dank underground cellar she called the Labyrinth. My head began to ache. Everything felt like a dream.

Finally, we reached a room papered with violet wallpaper. A massive curtained bed stood in the center, like a stage. A sad little chair huddled in one corner, and dusty lace curtains dangled at a single window. Housekeeper made a happy sound in her throat and ushered me inside.

"Here we are. This is your room, and I hope you like it. Dinner is in the Blue Room, and you'll have lunch in the kitchen tomorrow. Butler will come get you in an hour."

My heart leaped at the sight of the window. Other than the conservatory, it was the first one I'd seen yet. Adrenaline made my stomach curl and my fingers tingle. Maybe if I slammed something into it, hard . . . would they hear the glass shatter and come running?

Housekeeper was waiting for a response. I mumbled some reply, which seemed to satisfy her. After fluffing the pillows and dusting the edge of the bureau with a handkerchief, she left.

As soon as the door clicked shut I went straight to the window, but it was the solid kind that didn't open. I hadn't really expected it to just open, though. I ran my tongue over my teeth, thinking. Plan B, then. I needed to be quick in case they came running to stop me.

Grabbing the chair from the corner, I slammed the legs against the glass as hard as I could. The window didn't even make a sound. The glass didn't shatter, crack, or even shudder.

What?

I tried again. The glass held firm. I drew back, panting, and then swung a third time. The chair leg splintered, and I dropped the piece of furniture on the floor and slammed my hands against the glass. It only looked a few centimeters thick! It couldn't be that strong!

A sob caught in my throat. My eyes ached with fresh, unshed tears.

Why couldn't I get out? Magic?

Through the window, the sunlight was fading into the west. Dark shadows stretched across the lawn and hugged the tree branches. My father's truck was gone, and only the tire tracks in the dirt road gave evidence that he'd ever been there at all. I imagined him getting home, throwing open the front door and hugging my stepmother, my stepsisters. Showing them how the mark on his wrist had disappeared, how they were all free now.

I went back to the door. The knob turned under my hand, and I stepped back, astonished, when I saw the Hall of Regret with its horrible statues on the other side. That wasn't right. That hall was back by the room with the hourglass.

First the ballroom turned into a hallway, and now this. What was going on?

My heart began to pound again, and my stomach twisted with panic. I closed the door and leaned against it. The cool press of wood against my forehead calmed me. I could do this.

Be strong, Beauty. Be brave.

I counted my breaths until I was able to think past my panic. Then I straightened and opened the door again.

This time the room beyond was black as a nightmare. My hand slipped from the knob as I wavered.

I needed to get out of here. I needed to find a way out.

But I couldn't go back into that blackness alone.

Defeated, I shut the door and leaned against it.

I really wanted to cry.

FOUR

THE SERVANT HOUSEKEEPER had called Butler came to escort me to dinner. I jumped up when he knocked, my heart hammering. This was it. Dinner time.

It felt like my execution.

I opened the door. The servant was gray all over like a statue, and his skin was marbled with blue-gray veins. This time, I was able to stifle my gasp of shock at the strangeness.

Butler bowed stiffly, sweeping one hand ahead of him to indicate that I should come. His gaze flicked over me, and I wondered if they'd expected me to wear something other than the shorts and t-shirt I'd come in.

Tough luck. I wasn't changing.

He was waiting. Wiping my sweating hands on my shirt, I dragged in a deep breath and stepped into the hall. I could do this.

I would face the beast and demand to be set free. Demand to know what was going on. Demand that he explain himself.

If I could get any words out at all, that is.

Fear lay like a coiled snake in my belly.

Butler led me through a confusing string of rooms. A library, three parlors, a hall. Everything was old, heirlooms from another generation. Grandfather clocks and oil paintings. Chandeliers, strewn with cobwebs. Faded wallpaper, curling at the seams. Our footsteps echoed. I could hear my heartbeat in the silence.

Finally Butler stopped and indicated that I was to pass through first.

I stepped into a vast hall. A table long enough to seat fifty people filled the room, but every seat was empty, and its presence only made the hall feel lonelier somehow. Shadows crisscrossed on the table. And the room smelled like pressed flowers and dust. My heart thumped hard in my chest, and my palms sweated.

No Beast.

"Please be seated," Butler said, and his voice startled me with its nearness. "The Master will be here soon."

I just shook my head. I couldn't sit. What if I needed to run?

Butler pressed his stone lips together, displeased, but he didn't argue with me. He bowed again and left.

Cold air slipped over my shoulders and down my back. Wishing for a sweater, I picked up my napkin. My nervous fingers folded it into an origami flower, an old habit from my childhood.

It was late now—I wondered what Drew was doing. Probably homework. Or playing video games with a friend. I pictured his face, fierce with focus as he worked the game controller, the light from the screen flickering over his features. Was he thinking of me? He didn't know, of course, where I was. None of them did. It had all happened so fast.

I figured my father would tell them I went to live with my mother's family in the city. That was what people always said when their loved ones disappeared. They went to the city.

The door at the end of the room opened. My fingers stilled against the napkin.

He stopped just inside the room and looked at me. He stood with one hand resting against the doorframe. I inhaled sharply.

He was nothing like what I'd expected.

For one thing, he wasn't very tall. No scales or fur, either, or sharp jagged teeth to eat me with. He was just a guy. Black, thick hair fell into his eyes, which were a shocking blue. He might have been handsome once, but a long white scar split his eyebrow and ran across his left cheek, marring his otherwise pristine appearance. His lips were thin and pressed together tightly, as if in disgust. I immediately got the impression of rich, spoiled, would-barely-glance-at-me type.

And he was *young*. He couldn't be much older than me, which didn't make sense. The legend was from a time before my grandmother. I didn't understand.

We gazed at each other. Silence hummed in my ears and made my tongue feel heavy. Was he supposed to say something? Laugh like an evil villain, deep and throaty? Steeple his fingers and cackle? Tell me what he was going to do with me while chuckling suggestively?

Apparently, villains in my imagination do a lot of laughing.

He raked his gaze over me once. I felt like a package that had come in the mail, one in which the contents had turned out to be a slight disappointment.

"So you're the Curse Girl," he said finally, after a long pause. "The words of the curse spoke about a girl called Beauty, but I thought the line meant a beautiful girl."

I was trying to formulate a reply when the door opened and a girl entered. She was tiny, with soft blonde hair and exquisite green eyes.

"The Curse Girl!" She gasped. "Oh, she's adorable."

I thought this was kind of an odd word to describe me, since she looked younger than me. Maybe it was the whole rich thing. They thought they owned everything. I was just like a doll, or another piece of furniture. A pet.

"My name is Bee."

It was a stupid thing to say, and I immediately regretted it.

I'd wanted to sound strong, confident, and totally disinterested about the whole being-trapped-in-his-house forever. Instead I sounded like a little girl on her first day of kindergarten. *My name is Bee, and I like coloring and horsies.*

The dark-haired boy crossed his arms and smirked, like he could read my thoughts. The blonde girl glared at him. "Don't be such a cad, Will. Introduce us."

Will didn't say anything. The girl shrugged and looked at me with a warm, if slightly hesitant, smile. "I'm Rose, and this is my brother Will. It's really very nice to meet you."

None of the legends attached to the house had ever mentioned a sister. I didn't know what to say. Nice to meet you too? That was a lie. Curtsy? Um, no.

I settled for a nod, which seemed acceptable given the circumstances. Rose beamed, pleased. Will scratched his chin and looked at the door. An uncomfortable silence descended.

"Shall we sit?" Rose asked finally, gesturing at the table while shooting her brother a furious look.

Will pulled out her chair for her and then sprawled in his own without getting mine. Which was fine, of course—I was a capable, 21st century woman. Rose, however, looked scandalized.

Since nobody was really being forthcoming with the information I needed, I decided to just dive in.

"What are you going to do?" I wanted to say *to me*, but I couldn't. It sounded too brutal.

Will raised one eyebrow, his mouth sliding up in another smirk. "I'm going to eat my dinner. And no, it isn't you. I don't know what you've heard in your little village out there, but I'm not actually a flesh-eating monster."

Well, strike one against the village grapevine. I tried to look like I'd never considered this option. I probably failed miserably. Will's eyebrow shot up higher in disbelief.

"Really? They think I eat people?"

"Will," Rose said, reprimanding him.

He sighed and settled back, dropping it. Rose cleared her throat, and he looked at me with a falsely polite expression. "So what did you do, Beauty?" He enunciated my name like it was a joke. "People are very busy now, in the modern world, aren't they?"

"I'm a student. You know. High school?"

"I've heard of it."

I realized he probably had only heard of it, and wasn't just being snide. I didn't know what he was, but I knew he'd been here a long time.

Okay, maybe he was still being snide.

"I've never really gone to school," Rose said. She seemed determined to have a civil conversation, while Will seemed interested only in the opposite. I couldn't tell if he deliberately didn't like me personally, or if he just hated everyone. Both, maybe.

"What about you? What do you do?"

I needed to ask questions, draw him out. I needed to find out all the information I could. My voice sounded strong and smooth, but my hands were shaking. I put them in my lap so he couldn't see.

"I prey on innocent villagers and terrify their children," he said with a nasty smile. "And sometimes when I'm feeling really evil, I read books or paint."

"Will loves to read," Rose put in. That earned her a sideways glance. Then that sharp gaze was back on me, challenging me to confirm another village legend.

"I get that you're making a joke, but you preyed upon my father." I was getting tired of his sarcastic references to the town. We had good reason to be afraid of this place. Some of the legends were true.

My father was proof of that.

A muscle in his face twitched. His eyes, blue like lightning, rake across my face. Rose made a soft noise in her throat, like she was thinking of something sad. Neither of them said anything.

Just as the silence became unbearable, servants burst through the doors with steaming bowls.

Hands placed soup before me, some kind of bubbling yellow froth that smelled savory but unrecognizable. I dipped my spoon in it. My appetite had fled, but I needed to eat. I needed to stay strong so I could escape.

"That's pumpkin stew," he said, dismissive.

I tried the bubbling liquid. It tasted delicious, but I wouldn't tell him that.

"You never answered my question," I said. "You never told me what—what you're going to do to me."

He raised one eyebrow. "Do I have to do anything to you?"

"You called me the Curse Girl! You forced my father to give me to you! You must want something."

He gave me a look that made me blush all the way to my hair. "Not that," he said, disdainful at the very idea.

Jerk. I hadn't even implied anything like that. I ground my teeth together to keep back angry words. "What, then?"

"*If* you're the Curse Girl, you're going to help set me free from the curse I'm under." He returned his attention to his soup.

No way, I wanted to say, but I was supposed to be acting cooperative. "Well, what am I supposed to do? What am I supposed to say, accomplish? Pray tell, because I certainly don't like being here. I'd like to leave as soon as possible, and if breaking some curse will let me—"

He glanced up once, eyes bored. "Please stop talking. I'm trying to eat."

"Will," Rose said.

He glared at her so forcefully that she withered beneath his gaze and went completely silent. Will returned his attention to his soup, and Rose started eating like her life depended on it.

I got the feeling that he was like a big, nasty dog and she was like an annoying puppy, and occasionally she crossed a line and he snapped at her and then she cowered for a while and left him alone.

Now that it was quiet, I could get in a few words of my own.

"I gave up my entire life to come here —"

"I've seen what the village is like," Will said, his lip curling. "You barely gave up anything. You've only exchanged one set of chains for another."

Rage shot through me as Drew's face flashed before my eyes. I would never see him again unless I found a way to get out of here. I'd given up everything and everyone I loved to save my family even though they hated me, and he'd spit on my sacrifice with his callused words. I wanted to scream.

"You know nothing about me, my life, or the people I love," I snapped. "You really are a monster, just like all the stories say. You really are a 'Beast.'"

He didn't even bother to respond. He ate his soup.

Rose's eyes shot from me to her brother. Her lip trembled, like she wanted to say something, but she just put her spoon in her mouth.

Throwing down my spoon, I kicked back my chair and headed straight for the door.

He was a monster. Not a monster in body, maybe, but definitely a monster in soul.

He'd better not mind his curse too much, whatever it was, because setting him free was the last thing in the world I wanted to do.

FIVE

I FOUND MY room right away this time. Maybe there was a pattern to the changing rooms. Maybe it was all random. I didn't know. I didn't care. I stumbled to the bed and fell face-down on the blankets. I wanted to cry. My throat ached as if a giant hand were squeezing it. I threw pillows over my head and moaned.

The walls began to whisper my name.

Things rustled and stirred in the darkness above me. The bed curtains shuddered. The walls scraped and crackled like they were made of paper, and scuttling things were wriggling across them. Shudders worked up and down my skin. I put fingers in my ears and buried my head again, biting my lip to hold in a scream. I dragged the blankets over me as the muttering grew louder. Who was it? Ghosts? Spirits? Was the house haunted too?

Dimly through the hellish noise I heard something else.

Screaming.

It sounded like a man's scream. He sounded like he was in horrible, tortuous pain.

I put my head under the covers and closed my eyes. I didn't dare look for a way out tonight.

~

The sun woke me. I'd slept curled stiffly in a fetal position, a blanket wadded in my hands. My whole body ached. Uncurling, I climbed from the bed and looked around.

The walls, drenched in sunlight, were silent now. Did one of the painted flowers wiggle, or had my imagination started to get the best of me? My head throbbed.

Someone knocked on the door. Housekeeper. She bustled in without an invitation and started putting clothing in the bureau.

"Some clean things for you, dear. How did you sleep? Are you feeling well? You look a little pale."

She didn't look as frightening today. Maybe I had started to adjust. I watched, wordless, as she held up a mass of purple and black silk. A dress.

Housekeeper smoothed the bodice and toyed with the skirt, getting the lace ruffles to lay right.

"Isn't it beautiful? Seamstress made it last night for you. She has little else to do besides make clothes for the Master when his—" She laughed uneasily and broke off. When I didn't comment on the dress, her lips turned down. She put it on a hanger and hung it in my closet.

"Why are you called Housekeeper?" I asked. "It seems very . . . specific."

Housekeeper's hands fluttered to her hair, which was still piled on her head in an outdated bun. "We don't remember our names," she said after a long pause. "It's part of the curse . . . the forgetting part. We don't remember much of anything from before, except our duties and how to perform them. Do you still know your name?"

"Of course," I said. "I'm Beauty." I paused. That wasn't right. That was what *he* had called me. That was what the curse called me. What my father called me. But was that really my name? Mine?

My name was something else. Something loving, something my friends used . . .

The thought niggled in my mind, like a coin stuck in a crack. I bit my lip.

"Beauty's a nice thing to be called," she said, wistful. "*Housekeeper* is an ugly name. So plain and direct. Like being named spoon, or towel. I don't like it." She paused and leaned her shoulder against the wardrobe, reflecting. "I think I must have been called something nice once."

"Bee," I interrupted, remembering with a surge of relief as I remembered. "I'm called Bee. My mother came up with it when I was just a kid." My mother. Thinking of her made my throat close.

"Bee," Housekeeper said, brightening at the word. "That's a nice name too. Cute. Like a little Bumblebee."

I didn't know how much I would like being called Bumblebee, so I hoped she wouldn't find it *too* cute.

I tried to change the subject. "Couldn't you be called something else if you wanted?"

"Well, I suppose, but it wouldn't be mine. You understand? I want my name."

I nodded. That made sense. My grandmother always said there was magic in a name — significance.

"Wait — what about William and Rose? They know their names?"

Housekeeper shrugged. "The master is very strong-willed. He vowed he'd remember who he was if it killed him. But the mistress . . . they called her something else, before. But she's Rose now. It suits her."

I thought of her fragile skin, the visible veins beneath her cheeks. It did suit her.

Housekeeper opened the door to go.

"I heard someone screaming last night," I began.

She paused, picking at a piece of lint on her apron. "The house makes noises. The curse turned it into a great, mechanical instrument, a shifting puzzle box animated into something strange and terrible just to torment us. Sometimes the walls talk, but they don't say anything of consequence, just little whispers about the weather and things, echoes of words absorbed from the servants, that sort of thing . . ."

"It was very loud," I said. "Was someone in trouble?"

Housekeeper's eyes darted to the open doorway.

"I don't —"

"Was it the house? Was it someone he has prisoner?"

"No, no," she said, anxious now, as if I'd trapped her in a corner. "Now if you'll excuse me." And with that, she fled.

A servant with keys for fingers brought me breakfast and introduced himself as Locke. I nibbled at the toast while I made my plans. Today I was going to find a way out. If the windows couldn't be broken, then I'd find a door. A hole. A crack.

Anything.

I wasn't staying in this screaming house another night.

After eating, I explored. Daylight made everything a beautiful ruin again. I wandered through endless rooms, trying every window. Nothing broke. Nothing opened. I found no doors that led outside. Only doors that led to more rooms full of broken furniture and half-melted candles. My frustration grew, along with my sense of panic.

I came to a library, the one from before. Sunlight poured through a stained glass window and made a puddle of red and blue on the floor. Dust motes drifted in the air. Hushed silence hung heavy.

Stopping in the center of the room, I turned a full circle. Books lay everywhere in heaps. There were more books on the floor than on the shelves.

I picked up the heaviest tome I could find and hurled it at the window. The book crashed against the glass and fell to the floor with a thump. The window didn't make a sound.

I sank to the floor, my fingers groped for something else to throw—a book, a paperweight, anything. I found another book, but instead of throwing it I just held it, thumbing the pages with my fingers.

Maybe I needed something heavier than books and stools. Maybe I needed explosives. Dynamite.

Almost without thinking, I tore out a page from the book and folded it into an origami rose. The methodical act of folding and refolding calmed me. I thought of my grandmother. What would she tell me to do?

She would tell me to be calm and observant. I could learn the most from my environment if I wasn't panicking. Her blue eyes would smile at me and she would touch my hand with her own. She'd say, *Bee, you are the kind of girl who doesn't run from things. Some people call that stubbornness, and some people call that stupidity. But I call it tenacity and I think it's going to get you out of that house.*

A door creaked behind me. Probably Housekeeper, come to call me to lunch.

"What are you doing?"

I spun around at the voice, the paper rose in my hand fluttering to the floor. Will. Outrage was written in every line of his body.

"Can't I be in the library?" I snapped, because it was the first thing that came to mind. I couldn't say I was looking for an escape.

"You're ruining that book!" He pointed to the page I'd torn out. "That's a perfectly good book!"

Holding his gaze, I reached down and ripped another page out. "I'm making roses."

"Well, it's my book."

"Sorry." I tore out another.

He clenched his hands into fists. "This is my house, and I order you to stop. Don't you have any respect?"

I dropped the book, and it fell with a bang against the carpet. I folded another rose while I talked, my fingers flying. "None more than you do, apparently. How does it feel to be treated like dirt?"

"I don't know what you're talking about." His mouth made an angry slash as he scowled.

"Let's start with how you're a complete jerk," I said. "You told me I was ugly. You told me you didn't care about the fact that I've been locked up in this house with you. You don't care about other people."

"I'm cursed. Do you think I have time to care about you too?"

I finished folding the rose and let it drop too.

"Ditto, Beast."

He folded his arms. "I'd really rather you didn't call me that. I have a name."

"Oh? I thought everyone was just called by their most defining role."

"If that was the case, then you'd be called *Bitch*," he said. His shoulders rose and fell as he stood glaring. His eyes were very bright.

I refused to respond to that. I stalked out of the room, and he didn't follow.

SIX

I REFUSED TO eat dinner with them that night, although both Housekeeper and Rose came and begged me to come. I sat in my room and tried to think of ways I could escape the house besides just blowing it up, which wasn't going to happen of course.

Servants knocked on the door, but I told them all to go away. Eventually they did, and I was alone.

The sun sunk on the horizon, and darkness began to fill the room, drowning me in black. The whispers started, a cacophony of voices that hummed like bees in the walls.

And then the screaming began.

I crept to the door and opened it. A long, black hallway stretched before me. The screaming sounded muffled and far away. I shut the door and opened it again. Steps fell away from me, leading into the dark labyrinth I'd seen on my first day. The yells echoed weirdly, distorted.

It was coming from the labyrinth, then.

I didn't go down the steps. I might not avoid unpleasant things, but I wasn't crazy.

I shut the door and leaned against it, and stayed that way until morning.

~

"The Master has a message for you," Housekeeper reported.

I ran a brush through my hair at the dressing table. I didn't turn. "I don't want to see him or talk to him. He's a jerk."

She set down a stack of clean sheets on my bed.

"Please read it, Miss Beauty." She put a letter sealed with wax on top of the sheets and crept away.

Maybe I'd scared her off with my questions. After she left I picked up the letter. I wouldn't do what he wanted, naturally, but I might as well read it and see.

Dear Curse Girl,

I know you're interested in a way out. I know my sister likes to preserve a sense of decency and decorum, and that means dining with the guests, not matter how infuriating they might be. So to preserve the peace, if you'll join my sister and me for dinner, we can discuss your hopes of escape.

Your Most Humble and Obedient Servant

"Beast"

I crumpled up the letter and tossed it against the wall with a half-hearted sigh.

~

"You're not going to find a way out," Will said at dinner, after a cold silence in which the servants brought the food while Rose picked at her dress and her brother and I engaged in a scowling contest.

"Excuse me?"

"A way out of this house," he repeated. His blue eyes shimmered as he spoke. It was a crime how beautiful those eyes were. They made it easier to hate him, too. Attractiveness went hand in hand with villains in real life, no matter what the fairy tales said.

"Hmmm," I said.

"It's impossible," he said coldly.

"I'll believe that when I see it, Beast."

His face twisted with exquisite outrage, whether from what I'd called him, or my disbelief in his statement, I didn't know. "Don't you think I've tried to escape? Hasn't it once entered into your foolish head that if there was some easy way out, like breaking a window or opening the right door, I'd have done it years ago?"

"Well, forgive me if I don't trust you. You've got a nice setup here—servants you can boss around, a whole village that's terrified of you—"

He held very still for a moment, his shoulders rigid. The fork in his hand trembled. "Believe me, if I could leave this place I'd do anything to make it happen."

"As clearly demonstrated by your inclination to work with me."

He speared a bite of asparagus with the fork.

"You are infuriating."

"So I've been told. You'd get along well with my father. And all my high school teachers. Most of the people in the town, really."

"I doubt that. I imagine they're as pathetic as the last time I was there."

I wanted to slap him. But I needed information. "Yeah? When was that?"

He eyed me. "Long before you were born."

"How is that possible? How are you not like, eighty years old? You can't be older than twenty."

He lifted an eyebrow. "I'm not as old as that."

"How is that possible?"

"It's the curse. Time is different here."

That made me freeze. "Different? What do you mean, *different?*"

Will scowled. "I came under the bondage of the curse four years ago. But since then, more than a generation of villagers have come and gone."

I dropped my spoon, and it clattered to the floor.

"Only four years ago? Impossible." Still, my heart was pounding.

"That's all the time that's passed for me, in this house."

"You're just lying to scare me."

"It's true," Rose said. She'd been silent up until this point, watching our conversation with wide eyes.

I looked at her and noticed and feathery veins that patterned her face, the delicate blush of pink on her cheeks. Her eyelashes — were they . . . unfurling rose petals?

"Believe me, *Beauty*, I have other ways to scare you." Will's voice dragged my attention back to him. My skin prickled with sweat, and I looked away, thinking about the screams from the labyrinth I'd heard in the night.

Truth be told, I believed him. This house was crazy enough for it to be true. And if it was, then I had to get out of here fast. Otherwise I would break the curse and find Drew in college — or older!

Married, maybe. Middle-aged. He would be old, and I would be still a teenager.

My heart started pounding. I tried to calm down by taking a few deep breaths. I couldn't think about this now. I needed to focus. Get him to tell me more.

"How exactly is it different?"

"I don't know," he said. "When we — when the curse first took effect, the seasons passed quickly. Snow, spring, falling leaves . . . we watched it all pass by through the windows at a dizzying rate. But now the seasons are slower. It's almost as if the house were a giant top, spinning fast for three years, and now it has begun to slow."

Dizziness threatened to overwhelm me. I closed my eyes and took a deep breath. I would find out more about this time thing later. I had to prioritize.

"Let's talk about the curse," I said, trying to sound as if I were not about to become hysterical.

Rose sighed softly, as if I'd mentioned the death of her favorite pet. Will looked away. The muscle in his jaw twitched.

"Tell me," I said, and my voice came out sharp.

Rose flinched.

Will turned his head and caught me in his gaze. I wanted to shrink beneath it.

"There was a witch, and she cursed me. Cursed the whole house by extension, including my sister. She said there was a way to break it—if I was smart enough to find it—and then she left me with a riddle to solve and an hourglass to count down the time."

I remembered the hourglass from my first day in the house. There hadn't been much sand left in it.

"What happens if time runs out before you break the curse?"

His voice was icy. "Then I—we—remain cursed forever."

"And what about me?"

"I don't know about you. You probably stay stuck here too." He didn't look like he cared, either, which didn't surprise me. Why should he?

I needed him to keep talking. I couldn't figure out a way to solve this if I didn't know everything that was going on. "Tell me about this riddle," I said.

"Solve the riddle, break the curse. But I've never been able to figure it out. I doubt you'll do any better than me."

"Hey, you might try to contain your optimism. No reason to get your hopes up so high."

He scowled. "Do you always approach grave situations with such flippancy? You won't figure it out if I haven't."

I leaned forward and glared at him. "Try me, Beast Boy."

I expected him to refuse. Instead, with the sigh of an oppressed martyr, he rolled his eyes at the ceiling and recited the words, looking more like a boy dutifully repeating a school poem for his grandmother than the feared beast of legend:

Let the Owner of this House be Cursed
Darkness and Moonlight Change the Face
Unless the Brightest Pearl He Grasps
Forever, He'll take his Place
Creature of Regret and Scorn
Forever Left to Lapse and Mourn
His Fate inscribed in Letters of Love and Fury
Unless, Aid from a Beauty He shall Receive
Bestow the Long-Sought Gift and Then
Break the Curse With Word and Deed.

My skin prickled as I listened. I was supposed to give him aid? He was supposed to find a pearl? Something about moonlight?

"That's the whole riddle?"

"We've gone over every line dozens of times," Rose said. "Hundreds, maybe."

Will gazed at me, impassive. "And you have no idea what it could mean? Thought not."

"How can it? I just heard it. I need time to think." I hesitated, running over the lines again in my head.

"You really think I'm the person called Beauty?"

His lips tugged down. "Well, your name is Beauty. If that's what she meant."

"William," Rose said, warning him.

The comment stung. "If you want my help, you need to learn to be nicer."

"You want to break the curse, I want to break the curse. We don't need to be nice. We need to be effective. Just help me figure it out, and I'll make you a rich woman."

All I wanted to do was get out of this house. He could keep his money.

"Okay," I said. "We need to go through the curse line by line. Figure out what it means. The first part curses you, obviously. But that second bit, 'unless the brightest pearl he grasps.' Are you supposed to find a piece of jewelry?"

He sighed. "Believe me, I've torn this house apart looking for some kind of pearl. A pearl necklace, a pearl earring, a broach—anything."

"And?"

"I never found so much as a bit of pearl dust."

Crap. I fought the sense of disappointment that welled inside. Then I thought of something. "How are you sure it's in this house?"

"Well, how could I break the curse otherwise? The front door is locked to me. The servants can't leave. We're trapped here just like you. And another thing— the witch that cursed me used to live here."

"What?" That was something I'd never heard before in any of the legends in town. "She lived here?"

"Yes." He traced a circle on the table. "She was my sister-in-law."

"What?"

"She was married to my brother."

"I understand what the word means," I growled. "I'm just surprised. If she's your sister-in-law, why'd she curse you?"

"It's a long story," he said. "And it really doesn't matter."

"It might!"

"Look." He braced both hands on the table and leaned forward. His blue eyes snapped with unspoken emotion. "I don't really like having you here. And I don't really want you prying into the private bits of my life. So why don't you eat your supper and then go back to your room like a good Curse Girl, and I'll send for you when I need you to give me aid, whatever that might entail. Got it?"

"No way," I said, throwing down my napkin and jumping up. "I'm not some pansy you can snap into submission like Rose. I'm not going to cower — oh, the scary beast, what shall I do! — and forget about my responsibilities here!"

"*Your* responsibilities?" His hands twitched like he was keeping himself from grabbing a dish and throwing it at me.

"I'm supposed to help you break the curse, you idiot!"

"Listen," he said, his voice rising a little, "Just because the curse might mention you — and nobody is sure that's even what it's doing when it speaks of a beauty, mind you — doesn't mean you get free reign in this house, and it doesn't mean I have to listen to anything you say. Do you understand?"

"Fine." I scooted my chair back and stood. "Whatever."

"Where are you going?"

"To my room. You're being a complete jerk and I'm not going to fight about this right now."

"I'm being a *what?*"

I didn't respond. I just stalked out.

~

That night, the screams were worse than before. They rose above the whispers in the walls and the rustling beneath my bed. Did anyone else hear them? Was I going insane?

I lay on my bed with a pillow smashed over my ears to drown them out. But still they tormented me. Even the whispers in the walls around me didn't cover the sounds. Shivers danced up and down my skin as I listened. The words of the curse danced in my head.

Let the Owner of this House be Cursed . . .

I thought about Rose, and Housekeeper.

Darkness and Moonlight Change the Face . . .

The screams came again, dragging me from my morbid musings. I twisted under the sheets, trying to get comfortable. Trying to sleep instead of thinking about it. But I couldn't. Was someone hurt?

Was that horrible Beast torturing someone?

Someone like me, trapped here because of a malicious curse?

Forever Left to Lapse and Mourn . . .

Somebody was mourning right now.

I threw back the blanket and fumbled for the slippers Housekeeper had brought me earlier. I had to find out.

Feeling along the wall, I found one of the candles and plucked it from its bracket. The flame ignited once the candle was in my hand, just like before.

Slowly, I opened my bedroom door.

The steps to the labyrinth fell away from me. A dank draft caught the candle flame and made it dance.

"Maybe I'm supposed to go down these steps," I muttered aloud. Famous last words, maybe. I inched forward. My toe bumped on the next step down. My chest squeezed tight.

An agonizing scream echoed from below. I froze.

Better not go empty-handed. Who knew what was down there? I stepped back into my room and grabbed the candle bracket from the wall too. It was heavy brass. Good enough for braining monsters in a fight, right?

Maybe not, but I felt better holding it.

I returned to the stairs. Taking a deep breath, I began my descent. When I reached the bottom I put one hand against the stone wall and started walking. The candlelight illuminated only a tiny square in front of me. It was like walking into nothingness.

The scream came again, dying to a whisper before fading away into the blackness completely.

"Is anyone there?" My voice sunk in the darkness like stones in a vast lake. "Hello? Please, I want to help you."

I heard a rasping sound, a clink — chains?

"Hello? Are you a prisoner? Hello?"

I heard someone suck in a breath. Then they groaned, the kind of groan where you're grinding your teeth together to hold in a much more awful sound, like a shriek.

Apprehension rippled down my back like a trickle of cold sweat. Maybe this had been a mistake. There could be any number of horrible torture devices down here, just waiting for me to stumble into them. Maybe this was some trick of the labyrinth, like the whispering walls in my room.

"Are you hurt?" I whispered the words. I was afraid of the answer.

I waited for what felt like a thousand years. And then, I heard a voice.

"Who are you?"

"I'm called Bee," I said, excited to hear a response. I moved forward, looking for the speaker.

"Are you all right? Are you his prisoner too?"

He screamed again, drowning out the rest of my words. The cry died down into coughing. Gagging, almost. I came forward in alarm. "Are you all right?" I wasn't really good with sick people, like in an "I tend to faint at the sight of blood" kind of way, but I couldn't just let this poor guy suffer alone in the dark without doing something.

"Please," he said. It was definitely a male voice, raspy and strangled. "Please don't come forward. No light. It hurts my eyes . . ."

I halted obediently, shielding the flame with my hand. "Are you all right?" I repeated. I tried to sound calm and gentle, like a nurse. But my voice came out shaky instead.

"Everything hurts."

"Are you chained up?" I listened as he moved. Something rattled.

"Yes."

"You're a prisoner too?"

There was a long pause. "Yes," he said, like maybe he hadn't ever put that together in his head, and he was just now admitting it to himself as much as me.

"Me too." Excitement buzzed in my veins. If there were other prisoners in this house, maybe we could band together to search for a way out. Maybe we could fight the Beast and escape. I needed to get information from him. He could tell me so much, probably, like where Beast Boy kept his secret exit, or if the servants could be bribed.

I started with low-ball questions. "Have you been here long? What's your name?"

He moaned again. "Liam." It was more an exhale than a word. He sounded like he was dying.

"Are you really badly hurt? Is there anything I can do?"

In response, he screamed again. It sounded like someone had stabbed him with a knife or something.

"Do you want me to go?" I took a step back.

"It's not — so bad when — I'm distracted — " He inhaled sharply, like he'd been seized with sudden pain again. "It helps to — talk to someone — "

"Okay." I crouched down. I wasn't sure what the right thing to do was. My bedside manner wasn't so great. "Do you want to hold my hand?" That was something pregnant women did when they were in pain. "You can squeeze when it hurts."

As soon as I suggested it I flushed at the stupidity of my own words. *You can squeeze it when it hurts?* What was I, five years old? I stretched out my fingers anyway, and a moment later another hand grabbed them.

I winced at his grip, making soothing sounds. I wanted to ask him so many questions, but it probably wasn't a good idea right now.

"Do you want me to talk, then?" I asked quietly. "Or will the others hear us?"

"Please . . ." He panted. "And no, they won't hear. No one can hear. They're all objects at night, all of them. It's just me and you until dawn . . ."

The servants, Will, Rose, everyone? Night would be my best option to get anything done, then.

"I'm thinking of a way to get out of here," I whispered, excitement choking my voice. "I've been looking everywhere for a door outside — the one in the foyer is locked, but there has to be some way, somewhere — "

"There isn't," he rasped. "The whole house is sealed with magic."

"That can't be true." Icy fear flooded me anyway. No way out? I haven't believed beastly Will when he'd said it, but if this prisoner said so too . . .

No. It couldn't be true. I couldn't give up hope.

". . . Have to break the curse to escape," he said, sounding like he was speaking through gritted teeth. He was probably in pain again, and trying to hold in the scream so he wouldn't frighten me. His grip crushed my fingers.

The stupid curse again. I almost dropped his hand, but he held on tighter. "Don't go! I'm always alone at night. Completely, utterly alone."

"I — I won't." The agony in his tone broke my heart. At least I could make someone else happy in this miserable place, right? "I'll talk about . . . something nice. Okay?"

"Please."

I started talking.

At first my words barely made sense. I described the way the woods looked right now, with spring spilling from every branch and bursting up from the ground. I rambled about sunsets and the way cold water feels when you dive straight into a pool.

I talked my favorite books and my least-favorite ones. I told him about how my walls whispered at night, as if they housed a whole community of ghosts. I told him how much I wanted to escape.

Gradually his grip relaxed, as if the cadence of my voice was putting him to sleep. I talked until I was hoarse, and then I sat and let the silence wrap us up like a warm, black blanket. I could hear him breathing, low and steady. Finally he gave my hand a final squeeze and let go.

"Thank you . . . The worst pain is gone."

I got to my feet. "I should probably go. I'd get in trouble if they found me down here."

"Yes, you should go," he said. His voice sounded better now — not so raspy. But still strange, like he had swallowed rocks.

I crept away. My candle had burned down to a nub, and I cradled it in my palm. I found the stairs and climbed them to my waiting room. Slipping into bed, I shut my eyes and put my hands over my ears to silence the whispers, and I fell straight asleep.

SEVEN

I DESPERATELY WANTED to ask Housekeeper about the prisoner in the labyrinth, but I didn't dare. If anyone knew I was sneaking down there to collaborate with him, I'd probably be locked up at night too. But I wondered about Liam all day. Had he been forced to come here, like me? Had a bargain been struck with his family, had he sacrificed himself for their sakes? Or like my father, had he foolishly tried to take something from the cursed house?

I received my usual summons to join the Master and Rose for dinner. I grimly prepared for the ordeal, putting on my favorite pair of jeans and a black sweater. I felt fierce in black. I even threw on some of the makeup I'd brought in my backpack. I wasn't sure why I did it—it wasn't like I wanted to look pretty for that jerk, now was it? But before I could wash it off, the servant was knocking at my door to take me to dinner, and it was too late.

Butler escorted me again. I tried to sneak in questions about possible escape routes, but he wouldn't answer them. He wouldn't say much of anything, except "You'll have to ask the Master about that," which we both knew I wouldn't.

I fumed the whole way to the dining hall, which was long, because the house kept sending us in circles.

When I reached the dining hall and Butler bowed me through the door, the Beast was already waiting by his chair. Rose was nowhere in sight. He bowed, which I took as a sarcastic gesture.

"Beauty."

"Beast," I said, falsely sweet. It was a stupid comeback, but it seemed to annoy him, and that made me cheerful.

He cut a less-than-pleased glance at me when I called him Beast. But he didn't say anything. We took our seats, at opposite ends of the table again, and I stared down at my silverware while he toyed with his napkin.

"I'm glad you joined me tonight," he said.

"Save it."

"I'm trying to be polite to you," he snapped.

"I don't care about your fake manners," I mumbled.

He looked annoyed, but I didn't really care. He'd probably never had anyone talk back to him in his life except me. It'd be good for him.

"Where's Rose?"

"She is feeling poorly tonight. She's having dinner in her room."

"Ah." Well, then. I'd have to endure his company alone.

The prospect did not please me.

The servants brought our food, and we ate in silence.

When we'd finished dinner, the servants cleared the plates away and the Beast Boy stood. "If you'll excuse me—"

The last thing in the world I wanted was to talk to him, but the thought of poor Liam in the labyrinth pressed on my mind. I needed to find a way out, for his sake as much as mine. I needed to do something.

"Wait," I protested. "We should talk more about the curse. Maybe I can—"

"Why bother? You aren't going to figure anything out. I told you, I've been looking for pearls for years with no luck. I really doubt you'll be able to find anything I haven't, especially since I've lived in this house my entire life and you've just gotten here."

"You're really moody," I shot back. "And you're a jerk. And I'm sorry you have some horrible curse on you, but apparently you deserved it. And I didn't deserve to be locked in here with you because I didn't do anything to anyone. So why don't you take a Xanax and help me figure out how we can break this thing so I can leave before my boyfriend dies of old age without me!"

His expression changed slightly. "Boyfriend?"

"I bet it's impossible to imagine, huh? That there's someone out there I care about? That I came here because I wanted to rescue my family from the curse my father stupidly unleashed on us? Because I wanted to rescue them from you and the mark you inflicted upon him?"

His irritation faded into astonishment. "I didn't put the mark on your father. The curse put it there."

"What are you talking about?"

"Anyone can enter the house, but not everyone can leave. Your father made a promise so I'd let him go. He said I needed you, he said you were supposed to be here because of your name, because of the legends. He said he knew you'd come if he asked you—"

"No," I said, cutting him off. It couldn't be true. I had volunteered as soon as I heard the conditions, as soon as I knew what was at stake. My father hadn't—

But my father had known I would. Of course he had. He'd done this on purpose? I couldn't believe that. He would never do that. He would never . . .

"The stories of the magic hourglass are well-known in your town," Will said. "Aren't they? They say the sand in the hourglass preserves life, which by the way is a worthless fable. Many have tried to come for it before. Most never even got through the front door. But your father . . . somehow, he managed to get in."

A memory slipped into my mind. My father's face, twisted with guilt as he watched me walk towards the house. His eyes, avoiding mine. His hands, shaking.

Shock had immobilized me. I couldn't move.

Deep down, like the ache of a stab wound, I knew he was telling the truth.

"He begged me. He told me he had a daughter, Beauty, and that he would trade her life for his.
That he needed a bit of the magic from the hourglass for his wife . . . that she was dying, and he knew I needed a Beauty."

"And you let him do that? You let him just bargain with my life? Like I was a sack of potatoes? A used book nobody wanted anymore?" I struggled to breathe. I could barely get the words out.

Will scowled. "I thought it was disgusting and servile, but I was powerless. I stood there while he told me, and then I told him to get out. But the curse—it put the mark on him, and then I told him the truth. That it was a promise that he had only a few days to bring you or they would all fall under a curse themselves. But it was the curse's deal, not mine."

"What do you mean, the *curse* made a deal? It isn't a person."

"The curse took on a life of its own when it was pronounced on us, as all curses do. Do you think I have any control over the magic of this place? It does what it wants. And it wanted you. Your father knew that, too, somehow."

I was completely numb. My mind spun with memories—my father's eyes finding mine, his broken voice explaining that he'd gotten lost, that he'd gone into the house for shelter from the storm, that it had demanded he bring me back or it would kill us all.

I remembered the mark on his wrist, swollen like a bruise, pulsating with light just beneath the skin like phosphorous had slipped into his veins.

"He did it for her," I said, my lips numb as the realizations clicked into place. "My stepmother. She has cancer."

Was that a trace of sympathy on his face, or just disgust?

"He would trade his daughter's life for her recovery? What kind of father is he?"

It was hard to think. Hard to breathe. Hard to hear over the sound of my heartbeat in my ears. I'd been sold like a sack of corn. "I don't think I'm really his daughter. I know *he* doesn't think I'm really his daughter. My mother . . ." I didn't want to finish. I just wanted to cry. But there were no tears. There were never any tears.

I turned and left the room, and he didn't follow. I went back to my room and lay on the bed with a pillow pressed to my mouth.

When the screams from the labyrinth began after darkness fell, I climbed from my bed and took down a fresh candle from the wall.

Now it was my turn to need somebody to talk to *me*.

He'd been waiting for me, I think. His voice echoed in the darkness. He was panting softly, like he was trying to ride out the pain and failing miserably.

"Bee?"

"It's me." I crept close to him and then reached out for his hand in the darkness. "Are you in a lot of pain tonight?"

"Yes," he whispered.

"What's wrong with you?"

"I'm changing. Every night I change into a creature. An animal. Just like everyone else in this cursed place!"

His hand was hot in mine. A shiver ran up my arm. "A creature? Like . . . a werewolf?" Suddenly the chains made sense.

He hesitated. He probably sensed my fear. "Yes. Please don't be afraid."

"Will you hurt me?"

"No. I'm chained like a dog so I can't hurt anyone or break things. So I can't hurt myself."

That sounded horrible.

"Bee?"

"I'm here. How are you feeling?"

"It's not so bad now," he said. "It's nice to have company."

"Yes—" It was nice to have company. Someone to talk to who wasn't going to yell and snarl. My throat squeezed tight with unshed tears, and I drew in a quick breath.

"Are you all right?" Liam asked.

"No."

"Tell me."

His tone was gentle, despite being laced with pain. It uncorked emotion in me, and I poured out the story to him. I left nothing out—my father, the Beast and his horribleness, the crazy house and the whispers in my room. Drew. My friends. How I was afraid I'd come out and find them all fifteen years older than me.

He listened carefully. I could hear him breathing in the darkness near me, and it made me feel better.

"My father didn't want me," I concluded, giving a broken ending to my broken tale. Just saying those words felt like I'd swallowed a bunch of rocks. Hurt hung in my chest, weighing me down. My heart was one mass of raw, throbbing pain.

"Your father is clearly an idiot, because you're a brave, amazing girl. Right now you're holding the hand of a werewolf in the dark, just because he's lonely and in pain."

I squeezed his hand, and he squeezed back.

"I want to get you out of here."

"That's not going to happen," he said. "Not unless you break the curse."

"Are you dangerous if you're let free?"

He just squeezed my hand again. I wondered if he was a servant, condemned to this for some unpardonable sin like opposing the witch when she'd pronounced doom on everyone. I thought of Will—did he even care that Liam was down here, suffering?

"I'm trying to figure out what to do. The pompous jerk in charge isn't helping matters at all. I call him the Beast, which I don't think he likes very much."

Liam just laughed a little, and it sounded bitter.

He'd probably had similar problems with Will, I supposed. Especially if he were chained down here in the dark like this.

"Liam?"

"Yes, Bee?"

"Will you be my friend? I don't have any friends here."

He squeezed my hand again. I took the gesture as a yes.

~

"Good morning, Beauty." Housekeeper tiptoed into the room with a worried smile. I wondered if she'd heard about the conversation between me and her Master last night — was anything private in a house that whispered and muttered in the darkness, possessed by a curse that made deals with evil fathers about their daughters' lives?

I turned over on my side and stared at the wall while she filled up the water basin and fussed with the dirty clothes at the foot of my bed. I didn't want to talk. I didn't want to breathe.

"You must not blame the Master," she said after a long silence that she probably interpreted as me sulking. "He's angry a lot, because of the curse. He's changed since it happened."

"I should think so," I mumbled. It was hard to focus on anything except the feelings of betrayal that simmered in my stomach. "It's his fault."

"I don't remember the details," she murmured. "The curse, you know, interferes with our memories. But I remember him. He wasn't a bad person. He was a good boy. Kind, honest. Very friendly. But he's very angry now, very hurt."

Kind? Honest? I almost laughed, but I swallowed and it came out a sob. The curse must have really messed with her head. Thinking I was crying or something, Housekeeper drifted to the bed and patted my shoulder awkwardly.

"There, there," she said. "It will work out. You'll see. You're the Curse Girl. You're here to help us now."

"What I am supposed to do?" I burst out. "Am I supposed to know what I'm here for? The curse doesn't say. I'm just supposed to 'give aid.' It doesn't give any—" I yanked the covers back and shoved my feet over the side of the bed. "—Directions! Just some crap about pearls and moonlight and letters—"

I froze.

Letters?

An idea flared to life in my head like a struck match. I'd assumed—as had Beast Boy, I guess—that letters mean ABCs and such. Letters of love and fury, it said. But what if they meant letters as in paper? As in correspondence, as in instructions, or maybe even explanations?

I turned to Housekeeper. "Beast B—er, *the Master* said the witch used to live in this house. Where was her room?"

Housekeeper touched a hand to her cheek. Her thin mouth worked like she was trying to decide whether to tell me or not. "I don't know if I can . . ."

"Please," I said. "This will help him. This will help you. Don't you want to remember your name?"

"All right," she said. "Come with me while I do the dusting. I'll show you what it looks like. But I don't know when we'll find it. The house is very fickle in the morning."

~

To Housekeeper's surprise, we found the room right away.

"Maybe it wanted to be found," she said, surprised.

I took several steps inside the room. Dust lay over everything. A four-poster bed dominated the space and dwarfed a fragile-looking writing desk in the corner. Velvet curtains covered the windows, blocking the sunlight.

Everything seemed dead.

Housekeeper lingered. "The room's been sad ever since she left. Like the soul went out of it. I suppose you could say a room's soul is its resident, couldn't you?"

"I guess so." I needed to think. If there were letters hidden in this room, where would they be?

I started with the writing desk.

All the drawers were empty of everything but dust. My fingers left little trails in it, like tears. Something skittered away from my fingers in the recesses—a roach? I drew back, startled, and then I gritted my teeth and kept looking. I didn't have time to be worried about bugs.

I spent hours searching the book shelves and poking in dusty corners. The sun traced a shining path across the floor. Finally I sat back on my heels, exhausted and frustrated beyond words. I had spent almost all day looking and had nothing to show for it.

Maybe Will was right.

I glared at the sunlight playing over the floorboards. If only stupid time wasn't rushing past out there at quadruple-normal-speed or whatever, I would have a lot more leeway with this. But the sunlight just sparkled over the wooden slats, oblivious to my glare . . .

Wait a second. Sparkled?

I crawled over to the spot. Something glinted in the sun, a flash of metal. There was something shiny stuck in the floorboards.

My heart started beating triple time, filling my ears with a roaring sound. I stuck my fingernails in the crack, trying to reach it. This might be something important, or it might be a total bust, but either way I was going to get it out.

A shadow fell across my hand. I didn't look up. I was so close . . . the shiny thing slipped a little further away. I hissed in frustration. "Crap!"

"Housekeeper said you were in here."

I blew the hair out of my eyes. Will. He was the last thing I wanted right now.

"Is there something you wanted? Because I'm busy breaking your stupid curse."

"Oh really?" The scorn in his tone infuriated me, and I dug deeper for the thing in the crack.

"Because it looks like you're just pawing around on the floor."

"If you'll hold on a second, I'll show you . . ." My fingernail hooked the bit of metal—a chain—and I dragged it up and caught it in my waiting hand. A necklace? I brandished it at him.

"It was hidden in the floorboards. Maybe it belonged to the witch?"

He crouched down, cupping his hands around it. His eyes flickered with recognition, and the scorn on his face had evaporated into astonishment.

"Actually, yes. This was hers."

No pearls, though. My heart fell a little.

"Look," he said. "In the crack."

Paper. I pried it out with my nails and held it up.

"A letter." Triumph rose in my chest. See? I was useful. Apparently Beast Boy was too good to "paw around on the floor" and find things.

"Let me see." He snatched it from my fingers and unfurled the paper. I leaned over his shoulder to see, and he gave me a look that said he didn't like my being so close. I didn't care.

My dearest love, the letter began.

The Beast mumbled something under his breath.

Your last letter upset me deeply. I cannot tell you how saddened I am by your opinion on this most important matter. If we cannot agree on this matter, can we agree on anything else?

Last letter? How many letters were there? Which one did the curse mean? And what had they disagreed about?

I deeply desire your happiness, my love, but even more so I desire you to have goodness. If being happy prevents you from being good, then I'd rather you were miserable. Misery breeds repentance, after all.

"That's cheerful," I muttered.

He crumpled the letter in both hands and threw it across the room. "I don't want to read any more. This is sickening. She thought she could play God with other people's lives. She thought she could cast a few spells and that would fix everything. She was wrong. Her spells ruined us and turned her into a monster. Magic like that corrupts until the user is just dead and rotten inside."

I went to get the letter. "Is that what the curse was about? A lesson?"

"In a way," he said. "In a way it was revenge. I think she liked to pretend her motives were altruistic. It soothed her conscience if she thought she was teaching something instead of just punishing."

"What was in the last letter, the one she was talking about?" I asked, picking up the paper he'd crumpled and smoothing it out with my fingers.

"How should I know? I haven't read it."

"But you wrote it."

He stared at me. "No I didn't."

"You didn't?"

"No. That was Robert, my brother."

He took a step back and laughed in disbelief. "Wait, are you telling me that you thought this whole time that I—that I was the one who—"

He laughed again, bitterly. He rubbed one hand across his face and shook his head. "That explains a lot, doesn't it?"

"What?" I demanded.

"You think the curse was put on *me*."

"Wasn't it?" I thought of the house. I thought of the screams. Was the curse put on the house, the servants? It was on everyone. "You said you were cursed. I didn't dream it up!"

"Well, I mean, I am." He started pacing. "But it wasn't supposed to be me. It was supposed to be Robert."

"Her husband?"

"Yes."

I sat down hard.

This changed everything.

"Wait," I said, waving a hand. "But why are you cursed? Why is Rose cursed?"

"Here's the thing about magic," Will said. "It has a way of getting out of hand. She was really angry when she set the curse. It got too big and too powerful. It swallowed the whole house, and everyone inside. And once she'd done it, she couldn't undo it. And then after a while, she didn't want to. The magic ruined her too."

My head was spinning. So he hadn't . . . nobody here had . . ."You should probably tell me the whole story," I said. "Since I'm part of this lovely little soap opera too now."

"Soap opera?"

"Don't worry about it."

"Fine," he said. "I'll explain. When you join me at dinner."

"Why are you so obsessed with my eating with you?"

"Rose likes it."

I was so sick of his little traps, but I agreed anyway.

Because at least I was finally getting the story.

~

"Marian was in love with Robert from the day they met," he explained as we ate. The letter lay on the table between us. I was sitting on his right hand now instead of at the opposite end of the table. Rose was seated across from me. This way we could see and hear better. But it didn't mean we were starting to get along or anything. Absolutely not.

Will was getting into full-blown storytelling mode. His face was flushed and his eyes glittered with inner life. He almost looked like a normal person instead of a cursed recluse from a hundred years ago.

"Robert, on the other hand, has never been in love with anything but the sound of his own voice."

"Why'd he agree to marry her?"

"Well, Marian was rich when they made the arrangement. She later lost her fortune, and Robert began to lose interest. There were too many other girls for him to stay interested in one for long."

"That's sad," I muttered. Wickedly depressing, really.

"Our brother was a consummate cad," he agreed. "Anyway, Marian didn't know at first. Or didn't care. She loved him, even if his affection was waning. They were married in the town, and she lived here with us. She had her own suite of rooms after Robert began to drift in his attention."

"Was she, you know, a stereotypical witch?"

I wasn't sure how to ask if she was a horrible, horrible person.

He shook his head, looking puzzled. "I don't know what you mean."

Okay, so maybe *evil witch* wasn't a stereotype in his day.

"You know, was she cruel?"

His expression wrinkled. "No, not at the time. She was lovely." Rose nodded, her eyes downcast. I wondered if Marian had been like a sister to her at one point. What a betrayal that must have been. Of course, I could relate.

"Then why'd she put a curse on Robert?"

Will sighed. He cut a swift glance at Rose, who was staring steadily at her plate. He rubbed his hands together and looked back at me.

"Once upon a time, as they say, my brother, my sister, and I lived in this house. I was fourteen years old, and Rose was almost twelve. My older brother, Robert, managed everything after our parents died. He was ten years older than me."

I opened my mouth to ask a question, and he held

up a warning finger. "One day, a beautiful girl came to our door. Her horse had thrown a shoe and she was stranded. It was Marian, of course." He sighed. "She was the prettiest girl either of us had ever seen — her black hair was like a swath of ink down her back, and her eyes — she had the ability to look at you and make you feel like a prince or a complete idiot with one glance. Robert was smitten — he gave her his best carriage to borrow, and he saw her home himself. For the next several months he pursued her, and finally she agreed to marry him and they made plans to wed."

I noticed that his fingers had knotted up the napkin in his lap.

"A few weeks after their wedding, Marian found out that Robert was seeing another woman. She was furious — when she heard the account from the lips of the detective she hired, I thought she was going to stab the man. But she just stood there like she was turned to stone, and outside the sky turned black with storm clouds. Then she dismissed the man, turned, and went to her room. I found her writing a letter there —"

"The letter we found?"

"Yes, I think so. She stood when I entered, and she looked at me with those cutting eyes and she said she hoped I wouldn't turn out like my brother." He fell silent at that point, his chin in his hand. He stared at the candles on the table. I wondered what he was thinking about. Did he think he'd turned into his brother?

I waited for him to continue. The silence walled me in, brittle as glass—any noise I made would shatter it. I sat without moving until he stirred.

"Where was I? Sorry. She left that night. She wrote the words of the curse on a letter and left it in the front hall. I woke up to a pounding on the front door—someone from the town come to tell me my brother had dropped dead in a bar brawl at eleven thirty that night. I found the letter from Marian the moment after I received the news of Robert's death. And the curse, as all spells do, took effect at midnight."

"But your brother was dead—" It was beginning to make sense. My stomach dropped as I understood.

He met my eyes. "Yes. My brother was dead, and the curse fell on me instead. And because of Marian's fury, the curse was too powerful. It enveloped everything. The servants were bound, Rose too, and the house. And so we are all prisoners. Waiting for the day it will be broken. Waiting," he grimaced, "For you."

"I thought you said you didn't need me."

He rubbed his forehead. "I said a lot of things. I was really angry the other day, and sometimes I'm too hasty. You found this letter. You've proven yourself surprisingly insightful. Maybe we do need you."

I shifted in the chair. The tiniest trickle of good feeling, mixed with discomfort because I still didn't like him, puddled in my stomach. He'd locked up poor Liam, for instance. And he was a complete jerk. But . . .

"What happens to you all if you don't break it in time?"

His voice was flat but steady. "Then we become cursed forever, stuck in the forms we take at night until we die."

Rose put her hands over her eyes. Even her fingers had the rosy blush of new buds. Suddenly I felt horrible for her. She was just a little kid, really. She hadn't asked for any of this any more than I had.

Or, to be fair, any more than Will had.

"We want the same things," I said slowly.

"Are you trying to offer me a truce?"

I shrugged. "I don't like you. This doesn't mean that. It just means that I want out of here as much as you. And you've finally realized I could help you."

"So you'll quit storming out of here every night?"

"Only if you quit insulting me at every opportunity. And only if you start acting nicer. And only — " My heart pounded. "If you release the guy in the labyrinth."

Rose lowered her hands from her eyes. Beside her, Will tensed. "I'm sorry, but that's impossible."

"What has he done? Why must you keep him chained up like that?"

"Never mind that. It's none of your business." He put one hand on Rose's arm, because it looked like she was trembling.

"It's wrong! You shouldn't keep him a prisoner. He's in pain down there."

"Don't speak about things you don't understand."

"You're right. I don't understand. You should make me understand by explaining."

He stood. I could feel the anger rolling off him.

"No. I don't have to explain anything to you."

"What about the truce?"

"We'll work together to break the curse. That is all. Take it or leave it."

"What about Liam?" I faced him stubbornly. I wasn't backing down on this. "You're a monster to keep him down there."

He glared at me, but slowly the fury faded from his face and his shoulders relaxed. "He can't be free until the curse is broken, either."

I sighed. I didn't know if I could believe him. But we really needed to work together. I held out my hand. "I'll work with you. For Liam's sake. And my own. Not yours."

He took my hand and shook it. A shiver ran up my arm, and I dropped his hand as soon as the handshake was done. I didn't really want to touch him.

I was doing this for Liam. For poor Rose and the servants. And for myself.

Not the Beast.

EIGHT

AFTER I MADE my uneasy truce with Will, things
settled into a pattern. The days blurred together like
rain-soaked watercolors. Will continued to be a
regular jackass, and I continued to alternately fight
with him and ignore him. Rose, on the other hand,
was becoming more likeable every day. She had a
timid smile that infected me and made me want to
smile back. She began following me around, puppy-
like, as I wandered the house looking for ways out
and trying to think of what the curse riddle could
mean. When Housekeeper brought me lunch during
my searching, she started showing up to eat
cucumber sandwiches and drink tea with me. Will, on
the other hand, avoided me like a cat avoids water
(except for dinners, which he strictly observed).

On my own, I spent a week searching Marian's
room for anything that might be mentioned in the
curse, and I visited Liam every night in the labyrinth,
telling him about my progress and pouring out my
heart to him.

"I hate Will," I said one night as we sat together in
the darkness.

Liam's chains clanked as he shifted positions.

"Hatred is an ugly thing, Bee. It's like a muscle.

The more you exercise it, the stronger it gets. It corrupts the person holding it inside. Look what happened to Marian."

I didn't know what to say. I felt guilty now.

"What did happen to Marian after she cursed everyone?"

Liam sighed. "She's a shell of her former self. A twisted, ugly woman."

"She's still alive?" I vaguely remembered Will mentioning it. Why hadn't I thought about this before?

"She lives in the Fey Lands."

The Fey Lands?

"What's that?"

Liam hesitated. "You'll have to ask Will about that."

"Will hates me more than I hate him. He doesn't tell me anything."

"He's a broken person inside, and he's lashing out. I think he wants your friendship. He's lonely, you know. He just doesn't know how to ask for it."

"My friendship? I doubt that," I muttered.

Liam was silent, which is what he did whenever he thought I was being unreasonably stubborn.

"Fine. I'll try to be nice to him. And I'll ask him about the Fey Lands."

"Thank you," Liam said. "He needs it. I promise. Everyone needs love."

I supposed he was thinking about himself when he said the last bit.

I'd noticed how his screams and groans had diminished since I'd started visiting him at night.

Maybe his bit of the curse was getting better.

Maybe I was making progress somehow.

~

We were eating dinner. Or rather, Will and Rose were eating. I sat toying with my food, trying to drum up enough courage to ask him my question. He seemed to sense my trepidation, because he kept shooting me looks I couldn't decipher. Like he could tell I was nervous, and he wasn't sure if he wanted to encourage the feeling or soothe me.

Nervous anticipation slipped down my spine. I was just going to bring it up then, point blank. "If Marian is still alive, then why can't we just ask her to lift the curse?"

Will froze.

"That's a really bad idea."

"Why?" I demanded. I was sick of him making cryptic statements and never following up with explanations.

"It just is. Marian is crazy now. She's been completely corrupted by her magic. She won't do anything for us."

"What about me? What if I asked her? She doesn't hate me."

"She hates everyone," he said.

Silence fell. Will glowered at his food. I chewed my lip. I had another question to ask.

"What are the Fey Lands?" I didn't mention Liam.

"Oh!" Rose said, like I'd uttered a swear word.

Will lifted his eyes to mine, but didn't say anything for a long moment. I knotted my fingers in my lap. Had I said something very bad?

"The Fey Lands," he repeated, looking unhappy.

Rose seemed giddy, like I'd brought up a forbidden but secretly dreamed-about topic. "Will won't let me go there," she said.

"What is it?" I asked him directly.

"This house, once cursed, became part of another world. The curse binds it to the Fey Lands, a meeting ground for all things magical. It's why we're unstuck from time."

"And we can go there? I thought you couldn't leave the house." I didn't really know if I wanted this. I just wanted to try *something.*

"Technically, my house is now a part of the Fey Lands now, so the rules are different. But we can't stay in the Fey long, and we can't escape through it. We can only return here. But going there isn't a good idea. It's dangerous, and besides, Marian is there."

"Perfect. We need to talk to her. And I'm not afraid of the danger." I was totally afraid of the danger.

He shook his head. "It isn't what you're expecting. It's not a nice place."

"How in the world do you know what I'm expecting?"

"Trust me. You don't want to go. It's only going to depress you. And it's not going to fix anything."

First of all, he'd just thrown down a challenge. Second, when did he care about my feelings? I was suspicious. I crossed my arms and scowled. "I want to go. Now."

"Now?" One of his eyebrows arched up dangerously.

"Yes," I whispered.

"You'll have to change," he said, giving me a once-over that suggested my jeans and t-shirt were akin to beggar's clothing in his eyes. "Something more, ah, grand. Seamstress probably has just the thing."

Rose clapped her hands. "I'll help. You'll look beautiful. Just like a real lady."

Somehow I doubted that. But I didn't want to ruin the smile on her face. So I said it was fine.

Whatever.

After dinner I went to my room and dragged out one of the dresses in my closet. I gazed at the thing with a critical eye, and sighed and pulled it on. The fabric was black and lacy. The ruffled skirt dragged on the floor, and the bodice was so tight I could almost feel my ribs cracking.

"You look dazzling," Rose said with a dreamy smile. "Like an angry princess."

Grimly, I surveyed my own reflection in the mirror. I looked like a cross between Scarlett O'Hara and a Goth rocker chick. I ran my fingers through my hair a few times — not much I could do there — and went to find Will. Rose trailed behind, muttering about wanting to go too and how unfair everything was.

He was waiting in his study, the room with the giant hourglass. I entered quietly and stood at the door. Rose didn't follow. She knew where she was and wasn't allowed.

The hourglass sat on the table in the center of the room just as I remembered. The sand inside glowed faintly, mocking me with its glimmer. We had so little time left.

But it was Will who drew my gaze. He stood before an ornate, floor-length mirror, adjusting a button on his shirt. He'd slicked back his hair and put on a long black coat that made him look dangerous and hard.

When he caught sight of me in the mirror, he turned with a half smile. He looked startlingly handsome, and a shiver went through me. I made a mocking, half-hearted curtsy to hide my fluster.

"Hmm," he said, which was the only comment I got on my appearance. I resisted the urge to say something snarky back. Right now I needed to *not* get into a fight with him.

"Shall we?" He held out his arm, and I walked forward and took awkwardly. I'd missed my prom, but maybe this was a close enough substitute. All we were missing was the way-too-heavy bush of a corsage on my right shoulder and my stepmother taking too many photos while we posed on the front porch, smiling tightly.

"What happens now?" We were just standing in the middle of the room, in front of the mirror.

"Shouldn't we go through a door or something?

How do we get to the Fey Lands?"

Will glanced down at me, and his sharp blue eyes made me shiver. "We go through the mirror. Hold your breath. This is unpleasant."

He took a step forward, and I didn't have time to suck in air before we were falling.

NINE

WE WERE LOST in a fog. I couldn't see anything. At first my skin froze, and then it burned. Involuntarily I took a lungful of air, and it burned like I'd inhaled a mouthful of mouthwash. Cold and hot sensations scalded my throat and nose. Was I drowning? I thrashed, and arms wrapped around me tight.

"Stop struggling!"

Light and sound rushed around us without warning, and the ground sprang up like magic beneath our feet. Will had me in an awkward embrace, and he looked annoyed about it. I sagged against him, which was the last thing in the world I wanted to do. But my legs wouldn't support my weight. Over his shoulder, I could see a stone wall and dozens of people. A few were looking at us curiously.

"Stand up," Will said in my ear. "You're drawing too much attention to us."

I tested my legs, and they were working again.

"Sorry. I—I forgot to hold my breath."

He let go of me and stepped back. "You'll live. The barrier feels like ice and fire, but it won't hurt you."

I wanted to snap at him about how much "won't hurt you" had actually really hurt, but he offered his arm and I took it without speaking, because we had other things to do tonight besides fight.

Will leaned towards me.

"Just try to look like you don't hate me, okay?" He murmured in my ear.

I straightened my scowl into something resembling a smile. Then I got my first real look around, and my mouth fell open.

The room we were standing in looked more like a cathedral than anything else. Soaring ceilings were offset with sparkling stained glass windows that let in streams of sunlight. A lush red carpet stretched forward like a road beneath our feet. Mirrors lined the walls, and as I watched several people stepped through one, dusted themselves off, and started walking away. Nobody had the trouble I'd had.

"Why is the sun shining? It's night time."

"We're in the Fey Lands," Will said. "They're on a different time schedule."

"Oh."

"This way." He tugged at my arm, leading me forward. I craned my neck to stare up at the painted ceiling as we walked. Something fluttered at the top — I saw a flash of wings and scales.

"Baby dragon," Will said, following my gaze. "It must have gotten in here somehow. Don't worry — they don't produce fire until they mature."

"What is this place?"

"These are the Fey Lands. But they're not actually a specific land, mind you. Just a sort of a hub for passengers passing from one land to the next." His forehead wrinkled as he thought for a moment. "Dimension might be a word that makes more sense to you."

We turned a corner and entered another room, this one even larger than the first. Tents and huts spread everywhere like a tiny shantytown.

"The faery market," Will said. "They don't charge money here."

"No?" I stared at the rows of mysterious bottles for sale, the stacks of glittering silks.

An old woman with no teeth gave me a wide smile. "Want to buy a love potion, honey?"

Will steered me past her. "Her price might be your soul," he said, and his breath tickled my ear. I shivered—whether from the brush of his breath or from the idea of selling my soul, I didn't know.

We pushed through the crowds and wove around tents of wares. People of every size and description swarmed around us, some peering into our faces as they passed, some purposely not looking at anyone. I saw beautiful women with porcelain-smooth skin and black, opaque eyes that looked more dead than alive, short men with thick red beards tucked into their belts, slender girls with leaves in their hair wearing dresses of ivy and flowers. Men with pointed ears and long, feathery hair strode through the marketplace without looking at anyone. "Elves," Will murmured to me.

"They're very dangerous. Don't make eye contact."

I hastily looked away and spotted a group of young girls with tangled hair and olive skin that turned into scales at their wrists. Their fingers were talons.

"Harpies," Will told me in a low voice. "I told you this place could be dangerous. There aren't many laws or law keepers. Don't cause any trouble with anyone. Don't let anyone trick you."

"Does every possible magical creature hang out here?" I shivered as I accidentally made eye contact with a green-eyed, gray-skinned creature that might have been a goblin. Or a troll.

"It's a gathering place for anything and anyone connected with the Fey, yes. Many people disappear here. Many come to be lost, too."

His hand tightened on my arm as we passed a tall man dressed in a navy blue coat and a top hat. The man was kissing a woman's neck—at least I thought so until he lifted his head and I saw the trickle of blood that ran down his chin. The woman's eyes cracked open, and she gazed at us without seeing us. Will moved his arm to my waist and tugged me past at a faster pace.

I didn't even mind the extra contact, because my heart was thumping hard in my chest, and sweat had spread across my palms. I let him pull me away.

"Nearly every creature here is dangerous to you. Even the ones that look nice."

"Faeries are the worst. They look harmless, but they're vicious monsters. They steal humans away to use as slaves, or they suck out your life through trickery to make themselves look younger. Don't ever let a faery touch you unless you've made a specific bargain with him, otherwise he'll steal from you. The bargain binds him, and he'll hold to a promise, but you have to make them promise."

I nodded.

"Another thing," Will added, leaning close and speaking softly into my ear. "Don't eat or drink anything here, ever. You'll forget time completely and stay here a hundred years if you aren't careful. Humans like you are particularly vulnerable."

I nodded again, trying not to stare at a waifish girl in a red cloak who was arguing with a giant wolf-man. A curl of fear twisted in my stomach. Maybe this had been a mistake.

"William," a voice called out behind us. "William!"

We both stopped, and Will's arm tensed against me. We turned together to see a tall, dark-haired man with skin the color of burned wood and pointed ears weaving towards us in the crowd. Will relaxed, but only slightly. He kept his arm around my waist.

"Who's your lady friend?" The man asked, reaching us. His brilliant green eyes raked me up and down. His mouth cracked in a speculative smile.

"I'm Beauty," I said. I wasn't sure why I used my full name, except that it sounded much more formal than Bee. I was too frightened to be chatty. He exuded the energy of a thunderstorm.

"His Curse Girl?" He raised both eyebrows, and his smile stretched wider. Will sighed and didn't say anything.

"Storm," the man said, as if just thinking of the need to introduce himself. He bowed. "At your service, for a fee."

"He's a night elf," Will whispered. "A rogue one. He isn't as dangerous as some of the others, but don't trust him."

I examined Storm's face for any signs of bloodlust or capricious malice. But he only looked cocky, and maybe a little vain. His long black hair hung down his back in a mixture of curls and braids. The hat on his head sat at a crooked angle. He wore a necklace of dark stones, wrapped in string.

Storm pantomimed clutching his heart. "William, you wound me. You'll give me a bad reputation."

"You already have a bad reputation."

"Not with Beauty. Clean slate." He turned to me, licking his lips. "Don't believe anything he tells you about me. I'm very nice. Especially to ladies."

"Hmmm," I said. I didn't really like being referred to as a 'lady,' not when it was said with a leer like that.

"Skip to the point," Will said.

Storm flashed us both a bright smile, unperturbed by Will's belligerence. "I suppose you're looking for Marian?"

I was surprised, but then maybe I shouldn't be. Storm looked like the type who knew everyone's business.

He waited until Will sighed, reached out one hand, and touched the elf's fingertips. Then he dazzled us with another smile. "She's in the flower ballroom." With a tip of his hat, he pivoted on his heel and vanished into the crowd.

"That was interesting," I said. What had Will done? Had he given him something?

"You shouldn't have told him your name," Will said. He let go of my waist and offered his arm again. "Names have power."

"I thought that was only faeries and things," I said.

"You never know how long you're going to stay human in a place like this."

That comment chilled me all the way to my core.

Will started walking faster, and I hurried to keep up. My heart was thudding again at the thought of Marian. Even Will was comforting compared to her.

We passed into another hall and turned right, stopping before the third doorway. Above it swung a painted sign, covered with live flowers that sprouted straight from the wood by some kind of enchantment, probably. No words.

The flower ballroom.

"Not everyone here can read," Will said, nodding at the sign. "Shall we go in?" At first his voice sounded as harsh as it usually did, but then he looked at my face and his expression softened just a tad. "It's going to be okay. She won't, you know, eat you." Perhaps he'd seen my expression when we'd encountered the vampire earlier.

"Okay," I said, suddenly not wanting to at all and not liking the mental image he'd just given me. My legs shook a little as I followed him.

We were about to meet the witch herself. My stomach tied itself in knots. I dragged in a shuddering breath.

I needed to be strong, even though I felt like running. Or fainting.

The ballroom wasn't very crowded. Chandeliers hung from the high ceiling, covered in vines. Butterflies and birds swooped everywhere, and the scent of flowers filled the air. It would have been breathtakingly beautiful if not for an underlying current of danger that filled the air. Maybe it was just my imagination, or did every eye in the room immediately turn to us?

I felt her before I saw her. Her presence was like a strong perfume, overpowering and dizzying. I stood there, feeling her magic swirl around me like smoke, and then a tall woman with a swath of ink-black hair laced with silver turned to us, pinning us with her gaze.

"Marian," Will breathed.

Her skin looked too thin, like paper, and I could see all her veins, as if someone had cut her open and replaced her blood with a strange black liquid. Her eyes were black pools in the white mask of her face, and her clothing hung on her body limply, like a sheet caught on a tree in the middle of a rainstorm. The only color visible came from her lips. They glowed a deep, rose red.

"William," she purred. "How nice to see you. And who's this? Could you have found your Curse Girl at last, perhaps?" Her eyes dropped to me, making me shiver.

Everyone here seemed to know what a Curse Girl was, like it was a normal thing they talked about all the time. Then again, given the fact that evil witches were running around, maybe it was a normal thing. I didn't know.

"Marian," he said, inclining his head. His eyes were bright and hard, and I spotted a faint red flush spreading across his neck. "How *not* good to see you. This is Beauty."

Was I supposed to say hello? She gave me a hungry smile, and I just stood there.

"Oh, that's adorable," Marian said. Her voice was low and rich, like chocolate. "Her name is Beauty. How . . . tidy. I didn't mean that with the curse, but maybe it will work. These things tend to surprise even me, you know."

"Sure," Will said, careless and angry at the same time. "Listen, we came because Beauty here thinks you're a decent human being, and she thinks if she asks you, you'll tell us how to break the curse."

Marian's eyes widened in surprise, and then she laughed like we'd just suggested she give us a million dollars.

I would have expected her laugh to sound awful, like a mule's dying gurgle, but instead it bubbled up warm and infectious, the sort of laugh that made everyone else smile in spite of themselves.

It was an echo of her former self, I supposed. And then I just felt sad.

She'd been ruined by her magic. She was crazy.

"Tell you? First of all, that's hardly fair, my dear. The crow that is eaten doesn't cry foul to the hawk, you know."

I bristled. "Hey, cursing the wrong person is hardly fair either," I said. My voice came out wobbly with nervousness.

Marian paused, giving me a stare. Her face softened. "Your eyes, my dear, look like the surface of a lake when it's covered in mist. Your mouth is like a little slash of silk . . ." She dropped her face in her hands and began sobbing quietly. "He was so handsome, you know, wearing his ruined honor like a sword. He asked me why, you see. His voice trembled like a teacup in its saucer when he said my name . . ."

I looked at Will. He was scowling. What was she rambling about?

Marian's shoulders stilled. She raised her head with a snap, and she wobbled as if she'd just emerged from a dream. "My dear," she continued, answering my question as if she hadn't just gone off on a crazy ramble. "There is no 'fair' when it comes to curses. Do you know what happened after I cursed my dead husband and trapped his younger brother instead?"

"No," I whispered.

"Ah. Well, Beauty, I was with child. And when it was born, it looked just like Robert, that lying snake, and I—"

First her face crumpled like an old tissue, but then her expression smoothed out, and her eyes turned cold. "And I killed it. I couldn't have something that looked like that running around, could I?"

Her mood swings were giving me whiplash, and now this. I wanted to throw up. My arm started shaking against Will's. "You killed your own baby?"

"It looked just like him." Her eyes narrowed. "Do you understand?"

I felt sick. She was clearly psychotic, that was what I understood.

"You're not going to tell me how to break the curse, right?"

"Darling, you're brilliant." She blew me a kiss, and it came out like a puff of smoke and hovered in the air between us. "Will doesn't deserve you. Then again, he doesn't deserve anything but a dark hall and a cold chain around his—"

"Marian," Will snapped.

I snuck another glance at Will, and he was grinding his teeth.

"You're so handsome when you're angry, my dear," the witch cooed.

So she harbored an irrational hatred for anyone connected to her dead husband. How awesome was that. And I'd stumbled straight into the middle of this lovely family, and now my fate was wrapped up in theirs, and theirs was under the heel of a vengeful, crazy witch. A vein pounded behind my left ear, and my vision was starting to blur. I was so angry I wanted to slug her in the face.

"Beauty," Will said in my ear. "Calm down."

"You're a horrible person," I told her. My voice cracked.

Marian regarded me calmly, her black eyes impossible to read. "Curses don't hurt only the ones they are bestowed upon."

What did that mean? I stared into her face hard, trying to understand her expression, trying to make sense of her dizzying behavior.

"Beauty," Will repeated. He tugged at my arm, and I let him pull me back.

"The curse was for Robert," Marian shouted, at the last second before we stepped out the door. Her eyes opened wide, and she panted as if she'd just run a lap around the room. It was as if she had multiple personalities, each one surfacing for a few moments and then tumbling back into the dark recesses of her mind. This one seemed almost friendly. "The lines are personal references between the two of us. We used to write letters, you know. I loved him, you know." She put a hand over her lips.

Had she just given us a hint?

"I'm going to break this curse," I told her.

Her expression slipped from intensity into boredom. "Good luck. I'm not even sure I know how to break it. It's taken on a life of its own, you know." She yawned.

"Yeah," I said. "So I noticed. I hope you have trouble sleeping at night, knowing what you did to a sweet girl like Rose."

Marian just lifted her eyebrows and turned back to her drink.

Will dragged me to the first mirror he saw. The trip back wasn't as bad — at least I remembered to hold my breath the second time. My head was spinning with what Marian had said to me. When we stumbled onto the rug of Will's study, I picked myself up and turned to him in triumph.

"She gave us a hint!"

Will, on the other hand, was ashen. "That was a pretty terrible idea, taking you there. I shouldn't have done it. Marian is extremely unstable. Who knows what she would've done if she'd gotten really angry . . ."

"But she gave us a hint!"

"Maybe. You saw how she was. She's insane. And she said herself she isn't even exactly sure how to break the curse."

"Is that why she never lifted the curse after she found out it was you and not Robert who had it?" I asked.

Will rubbed a hand over his face. "First of all, anyone can curse someone, but once it's said and done the rules are binding. You can't just hastily pronounce a curse and then run around reversing things afterwards, and whatever she might have meant at the time, well, the magic can twist things to suit its own purposes. So she didn't lift the curse because she couldn't. And second of all, she wouldn't because the magic has made her crazy . . . Well, that and the fact that she loathes our entire family now. She killed her own child because it looked like Robert. She still wants me to suffer, just because I'm his brother."

I paced. "She mentioned letters. What she said to me — remember? She talked about letters."

He nodded, still distracted by his frustration.

"They wrote letters while she was away, during their engagement."

"Do you think maybe these letters mention some of the things in the curse? Like where the pearls are, for instance."

Will gazed at me for a full ten seconds before speaking. "That's the best idea I've heard yet. Well done, Beauty."

His praise pleased me more than it should, especially since it basically amounted to a pat on the head. What did I care if he thought I'd done a good job? Still, I smiled.

Will's eyes dropped to my dress, which he hadn't commented on before.

"You look very attractive tonight," he said. "A beauty and a Beauty."

Well. I didn't know what to say to *that.*

He didn't seem to know, either. He looked startled at his own statement. Turning away, he fumbled with something on his desk while I stood there struggling for a reply.

A knock on the door startled us both.

"Will? Beauty?" Rose's voice came through, muffled. "Are you all right?"

"We're all right," Will called. He gave me a look.

"We should probably talk about this in the morning. It's getting late."

I didn't understand at first what he meant. Who cared if it was getting late? We could stay up and try to figure out the curse. We didn't have a curfew.

Then it hit me. Oh right, the curse . . . at night . . .

"See you tomorrow," I said, feeling lame for not remembering. His comment about my appearance was still hanging in the air too, and neither of us wanted to meet each other's eyes. "And uh, thanks for taking me to see Marian. I know that must've been hard for you. With your history with her, and all . . ."

He nodded.

Feeling dumb, I let myself out and went straight to my room. I was so tired I forgot to go to see Liam that night. I fell into my bed and slept like a rock for the first time since I'd come to the curse house.

~

When I slept, I dreamed about my friends, eating ice cream in the summer sun. In my dream I was there too, watching them while the summer before our senior year disappeared like water through my fingers. They didn't see me, and I couldn't speak or even whisper to alert them that I was there.

I woke in a cold sweat, shaking.

The memories of such nightmares spurred me back to Marian's room the next morning.

I turned over the feather mattress and peered between every crack in the floorboards. But there was nothing to find. The room was empty as a water bucket in a drought. Finally, I gave up. If there were letters, they weren't in her room.

Will found me sitting in the middle of the room, dust motes floating around my head and tears running down my cheeks. He turned his head and looked down the hallway instead of straight at me, and I glared hard at a speck of sunlight coming through the window. The silence hummed between us. For some inexplicable reason, things were weird around him now. Unsettled.

He spoke first. "I . . . I want to show you something. To make up for last night." His dark hair was combed out of his eyes today, and it made him look older. Nicer, somehow. Like the kind of boy you'd take home to meet your mother. The kind of boy you'd get a milkshake with after school.

He helped me to my feet, and I trailed after him through the open doorway. We stepped into a long hallway lined with windows.

"Where are we going?"

"Just follow," Will said, his old self surfacing for a moment despite his good intentions. He opened a door and muttered something under his breath, grimacing. "If the house will cooperate, we'll be there in a minute."

The magic seemed willing. We only passed through the conservatory and three bedrooms before we reached the room he was looking for. The library.

I'd been here only once before, in the very beginning. Sunlight streamed through stained glass windows and made patterns on the rug. A few dried roses were scattered on the carpet in one corner, and they gave off a fragrant, musky scent. The hush of the book-crammed space enveloped me like a hug. It was lovely.

I remembered the last time I'd been here. We'd had a fight, of course. This was his secret hiding place, and I'd violated it with my stranger germs or something. This was his inner sanctum. But now he'd let me come here. He'd brought me here.

I could barely believe it.

"Soothing, isn't it?"

He was watching me like he was trying to figure something out. It made me vaguely uncomfortable, but I couldn't put a finger on why. Maybe I just didn't like being scrutinized like an exotic bird. Maybe I just didn't like him, no matter how nice he tried to be. To hide my discomfort, I ran my finger along the spines of a shelf of books.

"A lot of people think libraries are soothing," I said. Talking was easier than standing the suddenly awkward silence. "Books have a special magic, I think."

"Are you a reader?"

I shrugged. "Not really."

"Oh."

He seemed disappointed, so I hurried to explain. Why did I want to explain? I didn't care what he thought. Or did I?

"I like books, but I always got in trouble because I would tear out the pages and make origami with them. My grandmother taught me. My mother was so angry with her too, because I ruined every book in the house when I was small. My mother —" A painful prickle in my chest choked me, cutting off my words. What could I say about my mother? Words couldn't capture her essence. She had been everything in my life, and when she was taken away I had withered inside. I couldn't voice what I felt about her.

I made a helpless gesture with one hand. "When my mother died, it was like the sun stopped shining. You know?"

He nodded once, just a jerk of his head like he found the conversation a bit awkward. But his expression had softened. He seemed to understand.

We fell silent again.

I wandered to one of the windows, peering at the stained glass. The scene depicted a thunderstorm. Sunlight sparkled through the dark blues and the yellow lightning and made rainbows on the rug. It was beautiful. Many things in the house were beautiful, more beautiful than anything I'd ever seen in the town . . .

"What's he like?" He asked, breaking my reverie.

I turned my head. "Who?"

"This guy you're so desperate to get back to." He had settled in the one of the chairs by the fireplace, and he laced his hands behind his head, giving me a challenging look. He almost sounded jealous, but that would be ridiculous and he clearly wasn't.

Feeling defensive for no good reason, I grabbed a book off one of the shelves and started flipping through it to hide my flustered emotions.

"Be careful with that book," he said. "It cost more than your dowry."

My dowry. Hmmm. I decided to leave that little gem alone, and focus on the conversation at hand. But—we were totally revisiting that some day. A *dowry?*

"Drew is amazing," I said. "For one thing, he's the perfect gentleman."

Will's eyes sparkled like I'd called his mother something awful, but his mouth turned in a smirk.

"As I recall, my brother and I were the only gentlemen in the region."

Har har. "Not that kind of gentleman. I mean a nice person, not someone of noble blood."

He laughed. "Are you suggesting I'm not a nice person?"

"Are you kidding?" Now it was my turn to laugh.

He sobered when I didn't follow up the statement with anything else. "You're calling me a cad."

"Really, *Beast Boy*, your acting is excellent. I can barely tell you're joking."

"I'm not joking. I've been a perfect gentleman to you in every sense of the word, Beauty."

"Listen," I said. "You were an absolute jerk the first day I came. Can you deny it?"

"I—" He paused. "Perhaps I wasn't at my best that day. Your presence was unsettling. And it had been a rough night for me. You wouldn't understand."

"Try me."

He drew himself up stiffly. "I'd rather not."

I hated it when he pulled out the old-style crap. *I'd rather not* and such. He looked almost dignified saying it, like he was twenty years old instead of the right age to be in eleventh grade with me. He looked, well, like a gentleman. Not that I would ever, EVER tell him that.

"Maybe if you explained yourself more," I said, "We'd make a better team."

"Maybe if you pried less into my personal affairs, you'd find me more of a gentleman," he shot back.

"I'm not prying. Trust me, I'm only trying to break the curse and return us both back to normal."

His eyes narrowed. "No, you're not. You're trying to annoy and irritate me like you've been doing for days. I've decided your nickname—*Bee*—is completely appropriate. You're like an infuriating insect."

That snarky comment was the last straw. I snapped shut the book I was holding and stormed to the door. So much for bonding in his secret lair. So much for working together.

"Beauty," he called behind me. "Wait, I—"

I slammed the door in his face and looked around. I was in the conservatory.

I called him everything—jerk, monster, cretin, bastard, turd.

I ripped every single page from his precious book and made fifty origami roses with them. When I got tired of roses, I made a sailboat and a dozen birds. When the folded pieces of paper formed a pile beside me, I finally stopped.

My insides were throbbing, but the anger was ebbing away into something else. Sadness sucked at my soul. Why was I marooned in this awful house with Will and his curse while Drew and the rest of my friend lived their lives and enjoyed their junior year? Oh yeah, because I martyred myself for my father, who I now knew had betrayed me. Now I was going to miss prom. I was going to miss basketball games and sleepovers. I was supposed to start my first job working at the movie theater with Violet on the weekends. I was supposed to go to the lake with Drew, and be kissed under the stars, and . . .

Tears were splashing on the paper birds, making the paper wrinkle and soften. I stuck out one finger and stroked the nearest one like it was alive. I thought about my grandmother. What would she tell me now?

Be strong, probably. Well, I was sick of being strong. Right now I just wanted to be weak. Weak and weepy. I wished I had some ice cream to eat.

"Miss Beauty?"

Housekeeper stood in the doorway, her eyes wide and her hands tucked behind her apron. I scrubbed the heels of my hands across my face to get the tears off and then pushed up into a standing position. "I'm here, Housekeeper."

"The Master wants to know if you'll be coming to dinner."

I was not up to facing him at the moment. I was sorry about Rose, but she could deal with it. I couldn't. Not right now.

"No thanks. I'll be in my room."

She looked down. "Miss Beauty?"

"Yeah?"

"All of the servants, we . . . we believe that you are going to help him break the curse."

The words hit me like a punch in the gut. I'd been so selfish. This was about more than just me and Drew, or even Will. This was about a lot of people whose lives had been messed up.

"Thank you," I said. "And, uh, Housekeeper?"

She waited.

"Never mind what I said before. I'll be coming to dinner."

She beamed. "I'll tell the Master."

~

When I got to the dining hall, Will was waiting by my chair. Rose was standing at the door, trying to look like she wasn't listening, while he looked at me with a new expression in his eyes that I couldn't decipher.

We both tried to speak at once, and laughed nervously. He held up one hand.

"Allow me to speak first, please."

I nodded, letting him go ahead.

"You were right. I thought about what you said earlier, and I've been a true, er, beast. I've been a royal cad and a horrible host, and I am ashamed of myself. I've treated you terribly, and you've actually be really helpful to both me and Rose. Please forgive me."

My mouth had dropped open a little. I stared at him until I realized he was waiting for me to speak.

"Er, yes. I will. Me too. I mean, I've been selfish. I've only wanted to break the curse for myself. I forgot about all the other people involved in this. Rose, Housekeeper, Butler, all of them."

His mouth twitched. "You've been a lot less selfish than me," he admitted.

I shrugged. I wasn't going to get into an argument about who was more selfish. I just wanted us to work together so we could get out of this mess.

"Shall we?" He gestured at the table. I went for my chair, and he stumbled trying to pull it out for me first. I almost snickered, but held it in. I guess we really had a truce now.

"I know you're laughing at me."

"I'm sorry! It's hard not to sometimes." I looked up and saw he was almost smiling. Wow, he looked much nicer when he smiled. The corners of his eyes crinkled up and his mouth split to show straight white teeth.

He was really, really handsome.

I dragged my mind away from that idea. No way was that happening.

Will pulled out a chair for Rose, who had joined us now that the apologies were over. She beamed at me like I'd just handed her a million dollars. I noticed a few rosebuds sprouting in her hair. Were those new? Had I just never noticed them?

A sick feeling of foreboding filled my stomach at the thought that she was becoming more and more Rose-like as the days went on. Time was running out.

"So . . ." I gestured at her, trying not to look at the new flowers growing out of her head. "Did you tell Rose about what Marian said?"

"Yes. I told her about your idea, too." He sat beside me, picking up the bell to signal the servants and giving it a shake. "And I was thinking about the letters. Robert and Marian wrote dozens of them while she was away settling her father's estate. When she returned to marry my brother, she had those letters bound up in a book. I don't know what happened to it. It might be in the library somewhere."

I thought of the endless shelves. "Aren't there like, five thousand books though?"

"Twenty thousand," he said.

My mouth dropped open.

"We can find it if we work together."

I wasn't so sure. "Are we going to fight every step of the way?" I was still slightly skeptical about this whole apology-and-truce thing.

He gave me another charming smile. "Maybe. But I promise to be a gentleman this time around. By your definition."

"It's not *my* definition," I grumbled. "As if this is all part of my capricious whims or something. It's modern society's."

"Whatever. I'll be the epitome of it, no matter where it comes from."

I raised one eyebrow. "You aren't going to act like the Beast Boy I've known?"

"I give you my word."

I sighed. This was good. Really. We needed to get out of here. Working together was our only chance, wasn't it? And he'd been a lot nicer lately. Minus the smirking and the fighting. He'd been almost decent. Almost.

I sighed. Fine, whatever. I'd give him another chance, then. "Are you sure searching the library is the best use of our time?"

"Not really," he said. "But it's the only thing we've got right now."

Unfortunately, I knew he was right.

TEN

THE SUN WAS just beginning to brighten the horizon when I dragged myself into the library to join Will.

"Tea?" He held out a cup, which I accepted gratefully. The fresh scent of mint filled my nose.

As I sipped it, I realized I had never wondered where stuff like this came from, if we were all trapped inside the mansion. "Where does all the food come from? If nobody can leave the house, I mean. Does it come from the supermarket? Do you have a secret food-growing lab in the basement?"

"Magic. Part of the spell is that we're kept alive in here. The food is always waiting in the kitchen in the morning."

I took another sip of the tea. It tasted ordinary enough. "Magic food? Do you think you could request some mint chocolate chip ice cream for me, then?"

He laughed. "It doesn't work that way. The magic is impartial. Unknowing. It's just a force, like sunlight or air or water. It's not a person. It can't think."

"Oh." I frowned. "Then how does it know when we've successfully broken the curse?"

Will hesitated. "Magic isn't sentient, you know, but that doesn't mean it can't be set up like a machine."

I didn't understand, but I let it go. Magic was probably going to be as Greek to me as diagramming sentences. I put both hands on my hips and surveyed the rows and rows of books spines that snaked around the room, crammed onto every shelf. "Where do we start?"

"Anywhere you'd like." Will drained his teacup and set it down on a side table. "Look for anything that mentions Marian or Robert—not just the book of letters. A diary, a journal, anything handwritten. Anything that could perhaps offer clues about the curse."

"Got it." I pulled the first book off the shelf and started flipping. History textbook. Nope. I put it back. Will started searching through the books on the shelf above me, at the opposite end of the row. I tried the second book, but it was a guide to herbal medicines. I sighed.

This was going to take forever.

"So did you have any other brothers or sisters, besides Robert and Rose?" I asked. Anything to fill this deafening silence.

Will looked up from the book he was scanning. He closed it with a snap. "No. Just the three of us, until Robert passed. My parents are both dead too."

"Of course," I said, before I realized that although the curse had been cast more than eighty years before, for him it had only been four years.

"I mean, I'm so sorry." Oh, my stupid mouth. Sometimes I could be so thoughtless.

Will shook his head. He didn't look offended.

"They died when I was very young. I barely knew either one of them. Robert was both brother and father to me. He was my guardian, you see."

I was quiet, thinking about it. He'd been betrayed by his father figure, and I'd been betrayed by mine. We had that in common at least.

"What about you? Any brothers or sisters?" The moment he spoke a chagrined look crossed his face, like he was afraid he'd said the wrong thing by bringing up my family. He was probably thinking about my father and his abandonment of me.

"Don't worry," I said quickly. "I like talking about them. And yes, I have two stepsisters — Mindi and Jessica."

For a moment the only sound was our hands rifling through dusty pages. I thought about everyone out there, in the town. They might seem a million years away, but they were so close. Only a few miles. Did they think about me? Were they worried?

"They're pretty cool, I guess," I continued. "We fight sometimes, of course, and they don't talk to me at school. But I love them. I realized that for real once I came here."

He was watching me, maybe looking for some sign that the topic was going to make me sad. "I can tell," he said finally. "Your eyes lit up when you said their names. How old are they?"

"Mindi is a couple of months older than me, and Jessica is two years older." Just saying their names made my throat feel tight. In my mind's eye, I saw their long white-blonde hair, their big blue eyes, their smiles. And I missed them so much my whole body ached.

"I bet you really miss them." His tone was surprisingly gentle.

"Yeah, I do." A thousand emotions filled that single sentence. My chest tightened, and I swallowed back a sudden sob.

Will studied my face, digesting my sadness. He clasped and unclasped his hands, hesitating. "So you're the youngest." He said it like he was confirming a suspicion.

He was pretty clearly changing the subject to try to cheer me up. It was sweet. So I let him. I played along, scowling in mock outrage.

"What are you saying, Beast Boy?"

"Well," he said, innocently. "My brother always told me that as the younger one, I was doomed to dramatic displays of fury when I didn't get my way, and an insatiable desire for attention—"

He ducked, and the book I threw sailed over his head and hit the wall. "I'm teasing, I'm teasing!"

"You'd better be." But I was giggling. The laughter warmed me like a cheerful fire. How long had it been since I'd really laughed? Weeks? It felt like years.

Still smirking, Will grabbed the book I'd thrown

and flipped through it. He put it back on the shelf with a sigh. The cheerful mood faded back to seriousness again, like someone had flipped a switch. There were just so many emotions churning inside us both, I supposed. We were so morose today.

"I wish I'd had a brother," I said, after another short silence. "I always wanted a brother. Or a really fierce, protective sister. Somebody to look out for me at school when I was bullied . . ."

"You were bullied?"

"Of course. I mean, look at me."

"I'm looking at you. Am I supposed to see something that validates bullying?"

I made a useless gesture. "You said yourself that my being called Beauty was a mistake."

"I didn't say it like *that*, and we've already established I was being a, how do you say it? A jerk." He studied me, an honest up-and-down assessment. "And I was horribly wrong. You're very pretty, you know."

I buried my face in the book in my hands. Did he just say that? Awkward! "Uh, thanks. But the cheerleaders at my high school didn't exactly agree."

"Idiots." Will dismissed their opinion with a sniff.

"I think so too. But they were popular, and really pretty, and energetic. I'm not very energetic. Or popular. I'm more of a quiet wallflower type."

"No? I seem to remember otherwise. Especially last night. You yelled at an insane witch. And you've spent the vast majority of our acquaintance slamming doors and storming out of rooms. You seem pretty energetic to me."

"Well." I curled a piece of hair around my finger, sheepish. "But I'm not normally dealing with a crazy curse and a jerkish Beast Boy." I softened my words with a smile, and he looked up from the bookcase in time to catch it. Our gazes held. His blue eyes startled mine with their soft expression.

Something tugged in my stomach, and I busied myself with the bookshelf. What was that? Was my heart beating faster? Did I just feel a flutter of excitement?

No, no. We were simply feeling solidarity. A connection, a mutual understanding of two cursed prisoners. Right? Not *attraction.*

Hmm. That was a load of bull, and I knew it. I was attracted to him.

The realization made my skin prickle with cold sweat. I liked Drew. I practically loved Drew. I couldn't think about the incredibly handsome and — shockingly — sympathetic boy standing next to me. I couldn't.

As if in response to my mental panic, Will moved closer and leaned over my shoulder.

"What about your other friends — what were their names? You mentioned one named Drew," he said.

"Uh," I gulped. "He plays soccer and runs track. He goes to my high school."

"Are you . . . I'm not sure how it works now. Are you seeing each other? Courting?"

"Er, dating?" I shook my head. "Not really. Sort of. It's complicated." I wondered why I was telling him this. The words were just spilling out.

"Dating." He tested the word, and then smiled. "It sounds strange."

"Hey now. Weirder than courtship?"

Will ignored me. "What do modern people do when they date? In my time, Robert used to take Marian on carriage rides and walks in the forest. Or they'd sit in the parlor, or write letters to one another. Sometimes they'd go to plays."

"That's kind of like something we do, only a lot less boring stuff," I said. "Things like plays. Except they're movies. Do you know what movies are? Motion pictures?"

He pointed to a shelf, and I saw a dusty collection of newspapers. "They get delivered with the food. I'm not a complete idiot when it comes to everything that's happened in the last several decades. And yes, there were picture shows when I wasn't cursed."

Picture shows. He was kind of adorable. I swallowed a snicker and just nodded instead. It seemed the most diplomatic thing to do.

"So you go to movies when you're dating," Will prodded.

"Yes, movies. Restaurants sometimes, if we can afford it, or the park. Or bowling. But Drew doesn't have a lot of money. So we usually just hang out at the lake or at somebody's house."

"Doesn't have a lot of money?"

Was that a smirk on his face? It definitely looked like a smirk. So I rushed to qualify my statement, defensive about making Drew look bad in front of Beastly Will Moneybags, who had probably never had do work for anything in his life.

"But he works hard at one of the fast-food places in town, Burger Barn. It's new. For the longest time we didn't have anything, you know, being out in the middle of the woods like we are. You'd have to drive half an hour into Russville if you wanted to buy anything other than farmer's market produce. Now they have a supermarket and two hamburger places and an ice cream place."

I thought about that last bit for a moment.

"Mmmm, ice cream."

"Is it that good?" Will's forehead wrinkled as he watched my blissful expression.

"Ice cream? You've never had ice cream?" My voice shot up in disbelief. "I didn't think it was that new of an invention."

"It's not. But you said yourself the town only recently got an ice cream shop."

I shook my head. Apparently money wasn't everything. "Ice cream is the best thing you'll ever taste in your life. It's sweet and creamy and delicious."

We had steadily worked out way down the rows from opposite ends and now we were meeting in the middle. His hip bumped against mine as he reached up to pull another book off the shelf.

I scooted away. I couldn't tell if he noticed or not. His eyelashes flickered a little, but he was just looking at the book.

"Is there anything else you miss?" Will asked.

"My stepmother."

"Really? I thought—"

"That I hated her because of my father's betrayal?" He shrugged.

"Don't get me wrong—what my dad did was horrible. Horrible. I don't even want to talk about it. But my stepmother . . . you'd have to know her. She's one of the nicest people you'd ever meet. Her smile lights up the whole room." I imagined her, red hair strewn across her pillow like seaweed floating on a wave, her skin paper-thin and so fragile to the touch. The purple bruises that formed so easily on her these days. Her gray-green eyes, shut against the pain of her treatments. "And she was really sick, Will. Really, really sick."

"That doesn't make what he did right."

"I know." I grabbed another book and thumbed through it. My throat squeezed, making talking hard. "It hurts to think about how . . ." No need to finish that statement. Will didn't want to hear my sob stories.

I expected him to change the subject or let my words dangle awkwardly, but to my surprise he touched my shoulder. "I'm really sorry that it happened to you."

"Thanks." I looked from his hand to his face. My eyes traced the scar.

"How'd you get that?" I asked softly, before I lost my nerve. Since we were confessing all kinds of secrets today . . .

Will's eyes clouded over. "Marian," he said, the muscles in his jaw tightening.

I knew enough to drop it. We resumed our work, avoiding each other's eyes.

"Any luck?" He asked, after a short silence.

"Nothing. You know, this would be a lot easier if these books were sorted into some kind of order. I blame you, Will. It's your library."

"Duly noted. The lady wishes I was more organized in the past. Anything else you want to add? A dislike for my hair color, my height, my nose?"

"Being organized is a lot more controllable than a physical attribute — hey!" I squealed when he deliberately bumped me out of the way so he could get another book. I fell backwards onto the carpet in a fit of giggles. Will swung around, laughing.

A retort jumped into my head, but when our gazes caught I couldn't speak. The laughter in his eyes faded into an intensity. My brain stumbled.

Seriously, this was not good. I did. Not. Have. A. thing. For. Will.

Did I?

Will reached down to help me up, and when our hands touched an electric shock jumped between our fingers. I didn't know what to do or say. I wrenched by hand free as soon as I was on my feet and I took a few steps back.

"Jerk," I said, trying to tease him but sounding breathless and far too excited instead. My whole body flushed. I itched to move towards him instead of away. I put a hand to my cheek. Will stayed by the bookshelf, his blue eyes puzzled. I took another step back.

"Are you all right?"

"I think I'm going to go," I managed.

"Really? We haven't been working that long."

"Yes, but, I'm tired."

He looked skeptical, but thankfully he didn't push it. "All right. We'll work on it more tomorrow?"

"Tomorrow," I agreed, and practically fled the room.

~

"I think I'm attracted to him," I confessed to Liam. He'd become like my priest, listening patiently in the dark to all my problems and fears. He'd become my friend, offering advice and encouragement.

His chains clinked as he moved. He sounded almost amused. "And?"

"You're not shocked? Horrified? I mean, isn't it his fault you're a prisoner?"

"It's not his fault I'm here. It's the curse's fault. And no, I'm not shocked or horrified. You're a girl. He's a boy. These things happen."

These things happen. Um, okay. "Well, *I'm* shocked and horrified."

"Why?"

"Well, I'm sort of dating this guy, Drew. You remember. I told you about him."

"Your high school friend."

"Yes. Well, he's more than a friend. But not quite a boyfriend. And anyway . . . I like Drew. Not Will."

"So he's Will now? Not Beast Boy?"

I smiled in the dark to myself. "Oh, he's definitely still Beast Boy. But he's more than that too, I guess."

"It's progress," Liam said.

Sometimes I wondered whose side he was on.

ELEVEN

I WAS AWAKENED the next morning by a pounding on my bedroom door. I rolled over, squinting in the early morning sunlight.

"Whoizit?" My words came out gargled. Sleep clouded my eyes. What time was it?

"Beauty, wake up! You have to come see this!"

I rolled out of bed and staggered to the door. I put my lips to the crack. "Will?"

He practically knocked me over as he came inside. I realized too late that I was only in a tank and shorts. Probably way too much skin for an old-school guy like Will to handle without embarrassment. I mean come on, they barely showed their ankles in those days. But he didn't even seem to notice, he was so excited.

"Look!" He waved a handful of fresh white roses in my face. The scent tickled my nose, and I sneezed.

"Flowers. Very nice," I managed. I was too sleepy to puzzle through the reasons he was offering me roses. I just wanted to put my head back on my pillow . . .

"No, listen." He grabbed me by both shoulders as I tried to turn back for the bed, smooshing the roses against my shoulder. "These are *fresh* roses!"

"So?"

"There haven't been fresh flowers in this house in four years!"

"Not true," I mumbled. "There were roses in the library the other day. Can I go back to sleep?"

"Nope, you lazy bones, you have to see this first." He steered me for the door. I made a whimper of protest and pointed at the bed.

"Sleepy. Me. Bed. Now."

Will just pushed me through the door and into a musty study.

"It's, ah . . . very dark?" Actually, that was nice. I could sleep here, maybe.

"Not this room. C'mon." He crossed the carpet and threw open the opposite door. "Aha! Here we go." He swept one hand down in an elegant invitation for me to go first. I pushed past him with a growl. I was *sleepy*.

The noise died in my throat as I stepped into the conservatory and saw what all the fuss was about. My jaw dropped in shock.

"It's a boat."

A massive sailboat filled half the conservatory, the mast stretching up to the top of the ceiling and the hull resting on the flagstones like a giant wave had deposited it there. Mounds of white roses surrounded the boat and hung over the sides. I heard a rustle of wings, and looked up to see doves fluttering high above us in the sunlight, trying to get through the windows to the world outside.

"What the—?" A tickling sensation started in my brain. I was supposed to remember something. This was all very familiar, somehow. "What is going on?"

"It's some kind of magic," Will said, hushed reverence in his voice. He ran to the sailboat and rapped his knuckles on the hull. "Maybe it means we're close to breaking the curse?"

Realization rushed over me like a splash of cold water. "It's my origami," I whispered, stunned.

"What?"

"The other night I came in here after our fight. I folded a bunch of papers into origami. Some roses, a boat, some birds . . ."

He looked from me to the sailboat. There was no denying its existence. "This is unbelievable," he said. "This has never happened to me before, in four years of the curse. You . . . made these things appear?"

"I don't know," I said honestly. "I have no idea."

"That's never happened before?"

"Heck, no. But this is sort of my first experience with a cursed house too."

One of the doves landed on his shoulder. Will touched the feathers with one finger. "Did you make them docile, too?"

"I don't know. I didn't try to do it. I don't know how I would have given instructions to a piece of origami."

The dove took off again with a rustle of wings.

Will's eyes met mine. "Do you think you can do it again?"

~

In the library that afternoon, I folded roses and stars while Will searched through the books alone. I made boxes and lilies. I attempted a piano.

"I'm afraid I don't know how to make tons of things," I said, after failing to make a very good tulip. "I know mostly flowers. And boats."

"Don't make another boat," Will said, looking nervous at the idea. "It would take up the whole room. I really like this library, you know."

"Do you think the color of the paper affects the color of the object? I used blank white paper for the doves and the roses and the sailboat. And they're all white." I gazed at the piano in my hand, thinking.

"But those things are normally white anyway."

Will shrugged.

I looked around the room. "If we find some colored paper, we can experiment."

"Hey, look at this." Will dragged a book from the shelf, breaking my train of thought. "I think this is something we're looking for!"

I jumped up. My heart squeezed with hope. "Is it the letters?"

"It's a diary." He flipped through the pages. "Marian's. No letter. But who knows? It might tell us where the letters are. We should read it anyway."

I took it from him and flipped to the first page. *I have met the love of my life,* the first entry began.

"That's sort of tragic, considering how everything ended."

"Very," Will agreed. He put his chin in his hand and watched me as I turned the page. My skin prickling from his attention, I dropped my eyes to the written words. Marian's words.

Robert took me riding today. The fields were yellow with daisies, and the village children were playing in the creek. I've never experienced such happiness or such love. I shiver to think that I might marry this man, that our own children might one day play in that creek.

I skimmed through the entries while Will continued searching the library for the book of letters. Most of the entries were about the herbs she'd gathered or the spells she'd learned. Or Robert. A lot of the diary focused on Robert, actually. It was borderline ridiculous how obsessed she was.

"She really cared about your brother," I commented, after finishing another paragraph that described his flawless face and deep brown eyes.

"She writes about him constantly. And I mean, constantly. If you look up *obsessed* in the dictionary, you're going to find a picture of Marian and Robert."

"Marian was like a thunderstorm," Will said. His voice sounded muffled—he was crouched in front of the lowest shelf, checking the books buried behind a compilation of encyclopedias. "Her every emotion was amplified because of the magic. If she tore the hem of her dress, she cried about it. She was very passionate."

"Or psycho," I muttered.

"I felt sorry for her," Will continued. "She burned like straw — quickly ignited, but no endurance." He lifted his head to look at me, and I giggled when I saw a smudge of dust on his nose.

"You have a . . ." I waved my hand to indicate my nose.

"Where?" He rubbed at it with his hand and only succeeded in making things worse. I laughed. He was like a child sometimes.

"Here," I said. "Allow me." Will dropped beside me, and I wiped off the dust with my sleeve.

"Thanks." Instead of getting back up, he stretched out on the floor and folded his hands behind his head. His gaze flicked over my face.

"Marian was nothing like you."

"Not a workaholic kill-joy, you mean?" I lifted one eyebrow, pretending to be insulted.

"No," he insisted, serious. "She was beautiful and fiery, but she was insubstantial. And now she's completely crazy. But look at you. You're strong. You can still laugh after everything that's happened. That's probably the most admirable thing in the world. You do things. You don't give up. You're brave."

"Thanks," I mumbled, my teasing smile fading. At the moment I felt anything but brave. I wasn't a hero, and I wasn't admirable. I was simply stubborn enough to keep going even when everything seemed to be falling apart. My father had always hated that about me. He liked it?

"I admire you more than anyone else I've ever known," Will said. He reached up and tucked a strand of hair behind my ear. His hand lingered there. A shiver ran down my spine, and I looked away.

"I should, um, keep reading."

"Yes, of course." He dropped his hand. I went back to my place and opened the page back to where I'd left off. Silence filled the room like a flood. I was drowning in it.

I tried to think of Drew, but my mind kept seeing Will instead.

TWELVE

WHEN I SHAMBLED into the library the next morning, Will was sitting at a glistening white piano waiting for me. He didn't say anything, just spread his hands to indicate all the things that had changed in the night and grinned like he'd produced them himself.

"It worked," I mumbled, still astonished at the sight of the origami pieces transformed before my eyes. White flowers were scattered across the carpet. A sturdy-looking white box sat to the left of the piano. It looked large enough to store a bed inside.

"I can't quite figure out the size ratio," Will said. He played a series of chords. "The flowers are small, but the box is big. By the way, this piano is magnificent. Well done, Beauty."

I hadn't realized how much I liked hearing him say my name before now. I flushed. It sounded good coming from him. He said it warmly, like it was true. Like it wasn't some cruel joke played on me by my parents.

"Can you play?" I asked, to distract him from my blushing.

In response, he launched into a Mozart concerto.

I curled up on one of the chairs by the empty fireplace and closed my eyes, letting the music wash over me like rain. I almost wanted to cry at the sound. I'd forgotten how wonderful music was.

When the song stopped, I opened my eyes and found Will watching me.

"That was wonderful," I whispered.

He just smiled, and his smile was like the sunshine coming through the window above him.

~

The days changed far faster than normal. The tip of my nose starting feeling chilly when I woke in the mornings, and I began to wear sweaters to dinner with Will and Rose while we continued our search for the book of letters. Leaves began to trickle off the trees and cover the lawns in gold and orange, and the days began to get shorter.

I felt sick just thinking of all the time that had probably passed outside. I'd only been here for a month, maybe two — but it was already fall? I'd come to the house in May. Was it September outside? October?

Alone, I sat on the deck of the sailboat and watched the fall changes creeping across the landscape through the windows of the conservatory, and my insides ached. Were we ever going to figure out how to break the curse?

Will and I had searched through a little more than half the library with no luck other than the diary. I was still reading it, trying to find clues. But so far, I'd found nothing there either.

Things I'd folded lay everywhere. Roses as always, in fragrant heaps. Boxes, purses, shoes. A mirror. I picked it up and stared at my expression. I pressed my fingers against the chill of the glass. My breath fogged the mirror, making a circle. I drew a shaky circle in the middle of the fog and tapped two dots for eyes. A smiley face. But I drew a frown for a mouth.

Sometimes I felt as if I'd fallen asleep and never woken up. Like Sleeping Beauty, trapped in her bed for so long. I was living in a dream world, and like a nightmare, I was forgetting the people I'd left behind. I'd stopped seeing Drew's face every morning when I woke, in that dreamy space between sleep and waking before I opened my eyes. I used to think of him then, but now . . .

Was I forgetting him? The thought made my stomach hurt. How dare I let his memory slip away. How dare I betray him by my own apathy. It was like the lethargy of the house, stuck in time for so long, was seeping into my veins and corrupting my heart.

I slammed the mirror down so hard the glass cracked. A piece fell out onto my lap.

"What are you doing?"

I turned and saw Will in the doorway of the conservatory.

My insides tugged. He was standing in a shadow, his arm propped against the doorframe and his eyes on me. I closed my fingers over the shard of mirror and slipped it into my pocket. I pushed the mirror under a pile of roses. No reason to look suicidal or something. He'd worry.

"Hey," I said, glad to see him but afraid at the same time. This weird mixture of emotions had been cropping up a lot around him. It scared me – but I liked it.

"Are you all right?" He took a few steps towards me.

I looked out the window and then back at him. I thought about lying and saying everything was just peachy, but what would be the point of that? He deserved to hear how I felt. "No."

"What's wrong?"

A sigh rippled up from my lungs and leaked through my lips. Will hopped up onto the edge of the sailboat and swung his legs next to mine. I looked at my bare feet next to his sock-clad ones.

It was strange how different I was with him now. So opposite from the beginning of our acquaintance.

"What's wrong?" Will asked again, bumping my leg with his. "You're making your thinking face."

He said it to make me smile. But a tiny tug of my lips was all he got.

"Do you think we'll *ever* break the curse? I mean, honestly."

He was quiet for a long time, like he was thinking carefully about what he would say in response. I sat waiting while cold crept over my skin. Part of me wanted him to really think about it, sure, but a bigger part of me had just wanted him to say immediately *of course we will, don't be silly.*

But he wasn't saying that. He was thinking.

I stared at my hands and bit my lip.

"Have you finished reading Marian's diary?" He said instead of answering, after a long pause.

I let him get away with not answering, because I didn't want to hear his answer any more than he wanted to say it. It was easier to think of things to do rather than think of what we couldn't change.

"Almost. It's pretty slow reading."

"And no mention of the book of letters, or the curse, or anything like that?"

"Nope."

"You did skip to the end first, right? Because she might have mentioned—"

"I'm not a total dummy," I said, with a low laugh. "Of course I read the last bits right away. But the diary ends before . . . before this started. It ends with her wedding. Maybe she decided now that she was here with him, she didn't need it. Or maybe she started another one."

"We should keep our eyes out for it anyway."

"Yeah."

We both stopped talking then, and the silence rushed in like a tide.

This time it felt good. Being beside him was like sitting beside a warm fire. Comforting.

And right now I needed some serious comfort.

The prickle started at the back of my eyes. The itch of tears, unshed. I rubbed one hand over my eyes and cleared my throat. I just really wished I could cry.

"Beauty—" Will started.

I wanted to scream, but it came out like a sob. Will wrapped his arm around my shoulders and pulled me close. I pressed my face into his shoulder.

It was the first time we'd ever hugged.

We stayed that way for a long time.

"I'm scared," I muttered, my mouth mashed against his shirt.

"Why?"

"This stupid curse. We're not going to figure it out. We're not—"

"Yes we will."

I turned my head so my voice was clearer. "We need to go see her again." Meaning Marian, of course. Who else?

"What? Are you crazy?" Will pulled back and stared down at my face. He laughed in disbelief.

"The last time we went, it was a disaster. I never should have taken you. No. Absolutely not."

A thought popped into my head.

Who said he had to take me?

"Fine," I murmured, trying to look appropriately disappointed so he wouldn't suspect anything.

Will sighed and started to wrap his arm around me, but guilt was seeping into me again, and I moved away. He dropped his arm but didn't argue. He just looked at the floor.

"I'm sorry, Bee. I mean, we'll try harder to find the book of letters. That's what we need to do, anyway."

"Sure," I said. "You're right. We'll try harder."

But in my head I made other plans. And when the moon rose in the sky and darkness descended, I slipped silently to the mirror in his study that night while the house slept beneath its curse. And I passed alone into the Fey Lands.

THIRTEEN

EVERYTHING WAS AS bad as I remembered. Dark-eyed faeries sneered at me from behind a row of columns, and a thin gentleman in a red suit asked me if I wanted to give him my blood. I pushed through the crowds, looking for the flower ballroom. Maybe Marian would be there again.

"Beauty!"

I turned. It was Storm, the rogue elf. He caught up with me and, seeing that I was alone this time, flashed me a suggestive smile.

"No leash tonight?"

"I'm not under Will's thumb, if that's what you're implying," I said. "And go away."

"You're looking for Marian, aren't you?"

"I can't pay you. I don't have any money."

Storm laughed. "My dear girl, I don't accept money. I am paid in memories."

Memories? A shiver ran down my spine as I remembered the way Will had put his fingers against Storm's in exchange for information. He'd been giving the elf a memory? "What kind of memories?"

His eyes sparkled. "Ones full of emotion. They taste the best."

I thought about the night when I'd come to the curse house. The rage and pain I felt at being abandoned, the fear and sadness of being alone.

I wouldn't mind forgetting that moment.

"Okay," I said. I wasn't completely sure what I'd just agreed to, thought. "I'll, uh, trade you a memory and then you'll show me where Marian is?"

Storm tipped his head to one side. "Agreed." He reached for my hand. "Now think of the memory."

Closing my eyes, I pulled up the scene in my mind—the darkness full of whispers, the bed and the soft down pillows. My aching chest and dry, gritty eyes. Storm's hand burned in mine, and the memory was suddenly brighter, more vivid. I felt the pain burst fresh inside like I'd been slugged. I gasped, and Storm squeezed harder.

My mind went blank for a moment as the event I'd been picturing vanished from my mind to Storm's. The vivid scene slipped away, leaving a lingering feeling of sadness in my chest. And then . . . nothing.

"Ahhh," he sighed, and released my fingers. "Very good."

That was weird. I rubbed my hand and looked away. I felt like a mind prostitute or something. Hopefully that memory wasn't important, because it was gone now. "Okay, now where's Marian?"

Storm looked blissed out now. He blinked at me sleepily and licked his lips. "You'll find her in the Hall of Roses."

Awesome. "Well, where's that?"

"Sorry, I only give one answer per memory. If you want directions, you'll have to share another." He stared hungrily at me.

I wasn't sure at this point what I'd given him — my memory faded into a fuzzy gray fog when I tried to recall it — but I knew at least that it hadn't been a good one. I tried to think of another unpleasant situation, one that I wouldn't mind forgetting.

My arrival at the curse house?

No, I needed to hang onto that one. As awful as it was, I needed to remember that moment. I searched for something else. What about the time Will told me my father's true motive in bringing me to him?

My stomach twisted. Not that one. *Not one of Will.*

The desire to hoard memories of him surprised me. But there it was. I looked at Storm and shook my head slowly.

"Never mind. I'll find the Hall of Roses myself."

Storm frowned, but the expression shifted into something leering once more. "Fine. Suit yourself, Curse Girl."

I pushed past him for the faery marketplace. I didn't dare ask anyone else for directions. Storm had asked for a memory. Someone else might ask for my blood.

As I walked, it occurred to me that I didn't know how much time had passed. I was getting hungry, but I remembered Will's warning. No food or drink here.

Ahead, I saw a hallway of columns covered in ivy. Sunlight drifted down through glass skylights, and I could hear music. The scene was beautiful but surreal. Like being in the middle of a forest ruin.

Someone bumped into me, and I whirled, ready to defend myself if it were a vampire or a bloodthirsty elf. My heart stumbled in my chest.

But only an astonished young girl stood with both hands pressed over her mouth, looking equally terrified. We gazed at each other, determined neither was a threat, and then laughed together shakily.

"I'm so sorry," she gasped when she could speak again. "I was looking at the birds . . . I'm such a klutz."

Klutz? That didn't sound like something an enchanted being would say. That sounded like a human girl.

"You aren't a faery, are you?" She said, hesitant.

I grinned, relieved. She'd practically read my mind.

"Nope. Are you human?"

The girl beamed and clasped her hands together. "You can call me Anna. This place is so scary! I'm looking for a wizard named Maleus. Do you know who he is?"

"No, I'm sorry," I said, and I really was. I wished I could help her. "I'm looking for a witch named Marian."

"I don't know who that is," she said. "Sorry."

"Do you know where the Hall of Roses is at, by any chance?" It was worth a try, right?

A brilliant smile flashed across her face. "Yes, I do! Come with me!"

She stretched out her hand. "Here, take my hand and I'll show you."

I reached for her and then paused. What had Will said about touching people here? It was dangerous for some reason.

Anna tipped her head, confused at my hesitation. "What's wrong?"

Wait a second. A thought dropped into my mind like a stone into a pond, causing ripples of apprehension. She'd never answered my question about being human, had she?

"Faeries have to answer direct questions honestly, right?"

"Yes," Anna said. Her right eye twitched.

Suspicion hummed in my chest. I took a step backwards.

"Are you human, Anna?"

Her bright blue eyes faded to black as she hissed with fury. Only then did I spot her ears, long and pointed, and her fingers, with nails like claws. Had they been hidden with magic before? "Stupid human! I was so close to catching you. I hope you rot forever under Marian's curse."

My interest was piqued. "So you know Marian?"

The faery pouted. "Why should I tell you anything?"

I probably needed to bribe her.

I didn't want to give away another memory. That

was way too creepy. I chewed my lip, trying to think. What did I have? I dug into the pockets of my jeans, but the only thing I had was a piece of paper and the sliver of the broken mirror I'd put in the front pocket earlier. I pulled out the paper and folded it into a rose. Maybe she'd like origami.

"What magic is this?" The faery whispered. I looked down at my hand and froze. The paper rose had turned real.

"It's . . . origami." I was in shock. Apparently the change didn't need a night of magic to happen in the Fey Lands? "Here, take it. You can wear it in your hair."

The faery hesitantly slid the rose into her curls, and I pulled the shard of mirror out to show her.

"Anna" perked up when she saw it. "A shield!"

"It's a mirror."

She bobbed her head in a quick nod. Her long fingers were already reaching. "Yes, yes, a mirror."

"A shield against what?"

"Against magic, against mischief . . . it is nothing for you. Everything for me. I will take you to the Hall of Roses now," the faery said. "Give me the shield and I will take you."

Puzzled, I handed over the scrap of mirror. I didn't need it. Maybe it was a faery thing? The faery snatched it from me and tucked it away in her belt.

"This way," she said, pointing at the ivy-covered columns. "You will find the witch Marian there."

~

Marian was waiting for me. Someone must have told her I was wandering around asking about her. Maybe the faeries had a network, maybe Storm was being paid by her too, maybe it was just some freaky magic. Whatever. Either way, she knew. Her dark eyes raked over me, taking me in.

"You look a lot less pretty today," she said, sneering. "Less of a Beauty without your Beast, are you?"

"Never mind him," I said. "I'm here to talk to you. Just me this time."

"What do you want to talk about?"

"Don't play stupid with me," I said. "The hourglass is almost empty. We don't have a lot of time. I want you to give me another hint."

She stared into my eyes for a long time, so long I almost thought she'd forgotten I'd spoken. Then she laughed.

"Why do you continue to think that I am going to follow your childish assertions? I am not bound by you."

I moved in front of her when she tried to leave. My heart was thudding so hard in my chest I could almost hear it. "Because I think somewhere, deep inside, you're sorry about what you've done."

She went very still. "Girl," she said at last, her voice strange. "You do not understand the depth of guilt, do you? The agony of betrayal?"

"You don't know anything about me."

"Move out of my way before I cut you down."
Marian said, and this time her voice cracked like a
whip.

"Listen —" I growled.

"Beauty!"

A hand caught me and pulled me back just as
Marian began to lift her arm. I looked back, frantic,
but the witch had already vanished into the crowd.

"What do you think you're doing?" It was Will's
voice in my ear.

I shook his hands off me. "I'm trying to save our
lives, Will."

Incredulousness and fury waged war on his face,
and fury won. "Did you stop to think for even a
second when you were charging headlong into one of
the most dangerous places you could ever go?"

"I was fine." I would not be mentioning the faery.
Or Storm.

"Apparently not! I arrived just in time to drag you
away from an insane witch!"

"William," I snapped. "Stop. Just stop it. You're
not my father. You don't get to scold me like this."

He ignored me. "What would I have done if you'd
been killed?"

"Oh, I'm sure you'd still be able to find the book of
letters without me." My whole body felt flushed. I
was practically shouting.

"Bee!" He yelled. "Forget the curse. I don't know
what I would do if I lost you."

Oh.

Stunned, I looked at the floor, at his shoulder, any place but his face.

"I care about you, Beauty. This isn't about the curse anymore."

I held up my hand before he could say any more, before he could go some place we both would regret. "Please, Will. Can we just go home?"

He exhaled loudly and then scrubbed his hands over his face. His expression, when his fingers slid away, was resigned. "Yes, all right. Let's go."

But his eyes were wounded.

FOURTEEN

THE ROSES I'D folded over the last several days bloomed in vases all over the library, filling the air with their scent. Will worked at one end of the room and I worked at the other. I chewed my lip as I pulled books off the shelf and checked their interiors. Housekeeper brought us tea.

Was it just my imagination, or did her wallpaper skin look faded, like her real skin was showing through?

Hope swelled in my chest like a balloon, pushing away some of the sadness.

Maybe we were making progress?

The sun shone on Will's dark hair, making it look blue-black. The scar on his forehead glowed pearly-white. His skin seemed less sallow, his eyes less sad, although he'd seemed quiet and unhappy since we'd returned from the Fey Lands. Watching him secretly, I traced the shape of his shoulders with my eyes and memorized the way he wiped the dust from his forehead with the back of his hand.

How had I not found him attractive when we'd first met?

I ducked my head when he glanced my direction. I was so confused right now. He'd been on the cusp of a confession when I'd cut him off. Why hadn't I let him finish? What was I afraid of?

Oh, I knew exactly what I was afraid of.

The next book I pulled had a soft leather binding and no words on the cover. I opened it absently, still thinking about Will. My eye fell on the page.

My dearest Robert, I'm writing you this letter from my home in the city, and I'm missing you so dreadfully –

I froze. A roaring sound filled my ears, and my whole body went hot and then cold. I almost dropped the book.

This was it.

This was *IT!*

I tried to yell for Will, but my voice came out in a strangled squeak. My hands shook as I flipped through the pages. Hand-written letters, bound together into a book form . . . yes, this was it.

"Beauty?"

"The book . . ." I stammered. "It's the letters."

He was at my side immediately. He took the book from my trembling fingers. "You're right.

You're right! This is it!"

He grabbed me in a hug. I laughed, giddy and tingling, the weirdness between us forgotten. We'd done it. We'd found it.

"You're amazing," Will said, stopping and staring down at me. I gave him a smile of pure bliss. And before I knew what was happening, he bent down and kissed me.

I staggered back, my hand flying up to cover my mouth.

Will's eyes immediately darkened as he took note of my reaction. His smile vanished.

"I . . . I'm sorry." He said. He was breathing hard, not meeting my eyes. "That wasn't what I meant to—I didn't intend—have I upset you?"

I was trying to shrug it off. "Uh, no, it's fine."

Except it wasn't fine. I was pretty much freaking out at the moment. But more than that—

I totally wanted to do it again.

But I forced the thought away and tried to look casual. No big deal, right? He'd gotten carried away. We were just excited about finding the book.

The book. It hit me all over again. This was just too much, all at once.

"Beauty . . ."

I pointed at the book that was still in his hands.

"We should probably look at that." I couldn't talk about our tangled relationship right now. I needed time to think about it.

Will sighed heavily, then nodded. "Yes," he agreed. "Let's."

We both fumbled with the pages, laughed shakily, and tried again. My gaze fell over the first few entries again. "This was from a long time ago. What is there around the time of the curse?"

Will flipped to the back. "They end with her marriage. We'll have to read the whole thing." He tore out a sheaf and handed them to me. "Here. I'll take the first half, you take the last."

I blinked at him in shock. "I can't believe you just mutilated a book."

"Well, this book may hold the key to breaking the curse."

Good point. I took the pages and began reading.

He cleared his throat and started on the other half. I snuck a glance at him over the papers. He looked like he'd just lost his puppy or something.

I didn't know what to think.

~

When Butler escorted me to dinner that night, he didn't take me to the dining hall. We passed through it, but the room was empty and the lights unlit.

"Butler? Dinner?"

"No, Miss," the servant said with a mysterious wink. I noticed his skin was beginning to look more human just like Housekeeper's. "We're going to the Conservatory tonight."

Mystified, I had no choice but to follow him.

I sucked in a breath when we entered the conservatory.

Candles flickered on the deck of the sailboat, casting a soft glow across the windows and the mounds of white roses and lilies.

A blanket was waiting, spread with sandwiches and fruit. Violin music wafted on the air, and I spotted a servant playing in one corner. I turned to Butler.

"What's going on?"

Will stepped from behind the sailboat. "Thank you, Butler. That'll be all."

I gestured at the food and candles. "What is this?"

Will dropped his gaze. "I, er, thought we could have dinner."

I put a hand over my mouth. Was this an apology or a date?

"Please sit," he said, gesturing.

Part of me wanted to turn around and march right out the door, but Will looked so hopeful that I couldn't do it. I sank down onto the blanket and looked around again.

"Is everything . . . suitable?" Will asked, dropping beside me.

"It's very nice. But Will . . ."

"First, close your eyes. I have a surprise."

I almost didn't, but he looked so earnest sitting there. So I shut my eyes obediently. Nervous shivers were dancing in my stomach. What was he going to do? This was a mistake, right?

"Now open your mouth."

"Will, what — ?"

"Beauty," he said sternly. "Trust me."

I opened my mouth.

Something cold touched my tongue, and then I tasted a sugary burst of fruity coolness. Strawberry ice cream. My eyes flew open in delight.

"Ice cream!" I practically shouted it. "Where'd you get it?"

Will was triumphant. "Turns out, the cook knew how to make it. We have to eat it first, though, before it melts."

And so we ate ice cream on a blanket in the study, surrounded by candles. Will didn't mention the book of letters once. He was nothing but charming. I could almost pretend we were back in his time at some fancy party. He covered every acceptable topic of conversation for a stuffy old party — the weather (cold), my health (impeccable), the room (marred by a large sailboat). But he did it with wit and charm.

I tipped my head back to study the nautical monstrosity that had taken over half the conservatory. "You know, I like the sailboat. It adds a certain something to this room. I like to think I've enhanced the arrangement of the furniture with it."

Will just shook his head. The candlelight gleamed on his scar. When he grinned, he had a dimple on the left side of his mouth.

"I feel like I'm at a ball, almost," I said. "Ridiculous small talk, live music, candles . . ."

A devilish look settled across his face, and he stood. "May I have this dance?"

"Oh — I'm not a very good dancer," I protested. Suddenly my palms felt slick.

"Nonsense." He reached down and pulled me up into his arms. "It's not hard at all. Here, you hold your hand like this, and this—"

"I really don't think . . ." Being so close to him made my face heat up. I cleared my throat. "What I mean is . . . I don't know the steps."

"You'll be great," he said. "Ready?"

"I'm really not sure about this. I'm probably terrible."

But he was already leading me in time to the music, counting the steps into my ear. I stumbled, then found my footing. Will's arm tightened around me. My stomach was doing flops, but in a good way.

"Am I butchering the steps?"

"You're doing fine," he said. "You're not terrible at all. Quite graceful, actually."

"I took tap for two years," I offered. "Maybe that knocked some dancing sense into me."

"Not sure what 'tap' is. But you're a good dancer."

A smile tugged at my lips. Will touched my chin with his finger. "There it is."

The music changed to a slower song. I didn't know what to do, so I put my hands behind his neck and pressed my cheek to his shoulder. The standard slow dance, right?

Will stiffened slightly. "This is nice," he said, wrapping his arms around my waist and relaxing against me. "But it certainly isn't the way we would have danced at a ball. It would have caused a scandal."

I pulled back and looked up into his face. I'd never noticed how long his eyelashes were. Or the way the fringe of his hair brushed the tips of them. I liked it. "If you'd met me in your time, what would you have thought of me?"

"That you were the most beautiful girl I'd ever seen."

"No, really. What would you have thought?"

His eyes crinkled when he smiled. "I told you. Most beautiful girl."

"Liar," I whispered, but my tone was light.

Invisible threads tugged at my body, drawing me closer to him. I could feel his hand on my back, burning me through my clothes. I'd never felt this way about anyone before.

Not even Drew.

He brushed my lips with a kiss, and I felt the shiver all the way down to my toes. My head started spinning. Was I really kissing the beast of the curse house? And *liking* it?

I reached up and ran my fingers lightly over the scar on his forehead. I had never asked him how he got it. Will smiled slightly, turning his head to nuzzle my hand.

We kept dancing, and I fumbled for something — anything — to say.

"I've never danced with anyone like this," I told him.

"Not even your old beau?"

"Beau? You mean Drew?"

"Yes, I meant boyfriend. Beau was an old word for that. But whatever. The skinny, yellow-haired boy."

I shook my head. "No, Drew and I have never danced. We had no occasion to, because nowadays people usually only do that at prom and weddings —"

Wait a second. *The skinny, yellow-haired boy.*

I stopped dancing, and he stumbled into me. I stared up into his face. "How'd you know he was blonde? I never told you that."

Will's expression shifted. Was that guilt in his eyes? "Lucky guess."

No. No way. I had a really bad feeling about this.

"You weren't guessing, you were stating a fact. What are you not telling me?"

"This isn't the best time for this, Bee."

I stepped back, breaking his hold on me. "The best time for what?" A sick feeling trickled through my chest. I stared hard at him, trying to read the truth in his eyes. "What is it?"

Will ducked his head. "It's nothing. It's just that . . . It's — it's about Drew. He came here a few weeks ago. He wanted to see you."

"What? Drew came *here*? He came *inside*?" I could barely get the words out. All the air had gone out of my lungs. "He was here and you didn't tell me?"

"He didn't come in. He banged on the library window and demanded to see you."

My chest ached like I'd been punched. I wrapped both arms around myself. "What did you tell him?"

Will ran his hands through his hair, then covered his face with them. "I was so angry at the time . . . it was right after one of our fights. I told him you were here of your own free will and that I wasn't hurting you. He asked to see you. I told him no. He made some insinuations. So I yelled and told him to leave. And he did."

The aching feeling spread through my whole body. My next words came out in a whisper. "And you didn't tell me about it? You've been lying to me this whole time about it?" The ache throbbed as I spoke. I wanted him to deny it.

But he just shook his head sadly, confirming my fears.

"I didn't want to tell you. I was afraid it would just make you more upset. I was afraid—" He broke off and paced away from me, head down.

"What?" I snapped. Anger started to simmer inside me, eating up the aching feeling with hot flames of fury.

"I was afraid you'd forget about me if you saw him again." Will raised his head. His eyes were full of both pain and hope.

"You've made a huge mistake, Beast Boy."

Will flinched like I'd cut him.

"You've lied to me, and you've hurt me, and you've manipulated me with dancing and candlelight and all kinds of—" I broke off and covered my face with my hands. I wanted to scream. I'd been such an idiot.

"Beauty—"

"Don't even speak to me. I don't want to listen to your lying voice."

He went to the window and stared out at the darkness, hands clenched at his sides.

I drew in a shuddering breath. "I'm pretty angry right now at you. But I'm sure in the morning, after I've thought about this for a long time, I'll see some silver lining in all this. So for now, good night. Thanks for lying to me. You acted like a real friend. That was sarcasm, by the way. You've been a Beast, just like all the legends said."

Will wisely didn't try to speak again. I went to the door and yanked it open. Before I stormed out I glanced at him over my shoulder.

His head was down, and his face was contorted with sadness or anger. Maybe both.

I slammed the door as I left.

FIFTEEN

I SPENT THE next hour huddled on the floor beside my bed, trying to breathe. Will's betrayal cut me like a knife. I hadn't realized how much I'd started to like him, how much I'd thought he was a good guy. And now this? He'd lied to me. He'd hidden Drew from me. He'd been a first-class jerk.

I needed to talk to Liam so badly.

The sheaf of papers from the book of letters lay in a pile on my bed. I grabbed sheet and skimmed it, trying to take my mind off everything. The words blurred together, and finally I ground my teeth together and started folding. My fingers formed a shape with the paper while my mind ran over Will's words again and again. A key. I'd never made a key before. I stared at it dispassionately after I'd finished, then I dropped the paper creation on the bureau and began folding a rose.

I *was afraid you'd forget about me if you saw him again.*

"Not your call, Will," I muttered. How dare he try to manipulate my affections like that? What gave him the right to control me?

I seethed and raged while shadows crept across the windows and the sunlight faded into twilight. When the room was almost black, I grabbed a candle and went in search of the labyrinth.

~

"Liam?"

His breathing rasped loudly in the dark. He didn't respond to my call.

"Liam. Are you okay?" I crouched close to him in the darkness and blew out my candle. It would light again when I picked it up. He'd told me more than once that the light hurt his eyes, so I didn't take the chance of causing him pain with the lit candle anymore.

He grabbed my hand and held it tight. I squeezed back, trying to give him comfort. "Are you in a lot of pain tonight?"

"I'm all right," he rasped.

I scooted down next to him. I wanted to pour out my own story, but if he was hurting I'd pay attention to him first. "What's wrong?"

"Nothing," he said, but his voice hitched and I didn't believe him. His hand lay cold and clammy in mine tonight. "Never mind about me. You're upset, I can tell."

"Yeah," I said. The pain in my own chest throbbed. "Something horrible happened today."

"Tell me."

"Are you sure you're feeling okay —"

"Please, Bee."

I relented, or rather, the story poured out of me before I could stop myself from telling him. I almost choked explaining the events of the day — finding the book, my joy, the kiss, and then the revelation from Will that Drew had come to see me.

Liam was quiet for a long time. "That was a terrible thing for him to do," He said finally. "I imagine he's very sorry about it."

"It *was* a terrible thing! He should have told me! I can't believe he didn't . . ."

"And what are you thinking now?" Liam's calm voice soothed my frazzled thoughts. I sighed.

"I don't know. I'm really, really mad at Will. But at the same time I sort of understand. We weren't good friends when it happened. And what would seeing Drew have done for me? I'd probably just have freaked out or something." I traced his fingers with mine absently in the dark. "Maybe it was all for the best. But he shouldn't have lied to me."

"No," Liam said, and the word came out strangled.

I straightened. "Are you in pain again?"

"I'm fine. Really. Don't be concerned about me."

He sighed.

I stroked his hand, and the gesture seemed to soothe him. "I'm going to break this curse, and then you'll be better," I said. "Believe me, you'll be the one I miss the most when I'm gone. You've been a real friend to me."

"Bee, there's something I should tell you."

I barely heard him, though, because thoughts were suddenly crowded my head. Was I really going to leave? I'd been here so long I half-expected my skin to meld with the wallpaper like Housekeeper's. I felt a little like a branch, grafted onto a foreign tree. I'd begun to bloom, but now . . . now I just wanted to be cut away.

I just wanted to get out.

"Beauty," Liam said urgently.

I reached out a hand to see if he was in pain and accidentally grazed his face. My fingers brushed across fur, skin, a scar.

. . . A scar?

"Liam?" My voice came out unnaturally high-pitched. "What is it you want to tell me?"

A growing sick feeling had started gnawing at my stomach.

"Well," Liam said. "It's . . . er . . . Bee, I want you to listen to me — "

I picked up the candle. The wick flamed to life in my hands. I thrust the light forward, illuminating his face.

I saw a wolfish face, half human and half monster. I saw long, glistening teeth and electric blue eyes. Human eyes.

Will's eyes.

He scrambled back, hiding his face from the light.

"Will?" I gasped. But at the same time, deep inside me, everything was clicking into place. I'd suspected this. I'd known, somehow.

But that didn't make the utter betrayal I felt any easier.

"Please," Liam said. Will said. He was both of them. His voice was different, all rough and scratchy, but the eyes were the same. The scar was the same. It was definitely him, even though he looked like a monster instead of his normal self.

"Will?" I repeated. His name was the only thing I could say. A tremor went through my whole body, like an earthquake of emotion. I just sat there paralyzed, holding the candle over him, my arm shaking. Wax dripped down my arm.

"Beauty, please—listen to me."

I scooted backwards, shaking my head. This was too much. First Drew, now this—what else had he lied about?

"Listen! I couldn't tell you at first because—because you'd have run away! Look at me! I'm a werewolf! I'm chained up down here at night because I'm dangerous. You want to see the beast of legend? This is the beast. This is me, cursed!" He drew in a sobbing breath. His eyes were bright, feverish. The words kept spilling out of him, a waterfall of desperate explanations. "I was so lonely, because everyone else was afraid of me when I was like this, and you weren't . . . and then I didn't tell you because I didn't know how. I wanted you to be my friend. And then when you were my friend, I didn't want to lose you. You hated Will, but you didn't hate me." His voice broke over the last bit.

Fresh pain exploded inside me. "If you wanted to be my friend, you should have told me the truth instead of lying and manipulating me. That's like, Friendship 101 stuff!"

"I am so sorry," he said, his face twisting with pain. He looked like a wounded animal.

Something inside me hardened into a tight, cold ball. "It's a little late for that." I rose to my feet.

"Beauty," he rasped. The chains jangled as he jerked against them violently. "Where are you going?"

"I don't know. Some place without you in it."

He yelled my name again, but I didn't stop until I'd gotten back to my room.

Halfway there, I realized I was crying for the first time since my mother had left me. His betrayal had uncorked a powerful emotion inside the deepest corners of my inner self. It hurt so bad I doubled over on the floor of my room, dropping the candle. Nobody had ever hurt me this way before, not even my father when he'd left me here, because my father had never loved me or cared about me.

Not like Will.

I curled up in the middle of my bed and cried myself to sleep.

~

I woke before it was light. I uncurled slowly, stretching my stiffened limbs and moaning as blood rushed into my extremities. My throat was scratchy and dry, like I'd swallowed a fistful of leaves, and my head throbbed. At first I didn't understand what had happened, and except for a dull ache in my chest I felt almost normal.

And then everything hit me like a splash of icy water. Last night. The fight. The revelation. Will had lied about Drew. Will had lied about being Liam.

Was there anything Will hadn't lied about?

I sat up in my bed, fumbling for something to fold so I could calm down. My fingers closed over cold metal. A key? I vaguely remembered making it the night before, when I had been so distressed. What good was a stupid key? I needed a baseball bat, or a crowbar. Something I could use to smash every breakable thing in this house.

I slid out of the bed and dragged on a coat, the key still clasped in my fingers. Someone knocked on the door, probably Housekeeper, but I ignored them, and eventually the person slid something under the door and went away.

An envelope. Probably more explanations from Will. I glared at it, not wanting to pick it up.

I didn't want to speak to him right now. Ever, maybe. It was hard to think through the fog in my head.

The key was heavy in my hand. I looked down at it, and an idea began to form. I almost sobbed when I thought of it. Impossible . . . right?

Grabbing my backpack, I stuffed everything I'd brought to the curse house inside. My clothes, my toiletries, my hairbrush. The things that I'd brought with me. The things that were mine.

I left the things he'd given me, the things Seamstress had made me, the things I'd made myself from paper. Except the key. That went into my pocket. I got dressed quickly, my breathing quick and heavy in the stillness. Hope began to blossom in my chest.

This might work.

When I was finished, I tiptoed to the door and slipped out.

The house was still in the pre-dawn darkness. The glimmer of light shimmered at the windows, signaling sunrise. I moved noiselessly across the carpeted floors, slipping up and down staircases and through studies and halls. Finally I found the foyer.

I hadn't been back since the day I'd come. Everything was the same — the overturned furniture, the scattered papers. The heavy oak door with the brass knob.

Everything else faded into a blur around me. Slowly I crept forward. My heart struggled in my chest. Hope made me dizzy. I pulled the key from my pocket and slid it with a clink into the keyhole.

My pulse crashed in my ears. My fingers were numb.

I turned the key.

Click.
The door opened.
I was free.

SIXTEEN

I LEFT WITHOUT looking back. I ran all the way across the lawn. Dew soaked my socks and bits of wet grass clung to my legs. I kept running into the woods while the tears streamed down my face. My lungs ached and my nose burned, but I didn't stop.

I ran all the way home. I wanted to see Drew first, and my other friends, but I ached for my stepsisters and I needed to see my father.

There were no words in my mouth for him. But I needed to see him anyway.

When I reached our street a fresh burst of energy filled me, propelling me forward. The sun had risen and cars were rumbling past — people were on their way to work, or school, or something. I realized I didn't know what day it was, what month it was. The air was cold and crisp, and the tree branches were mostly bare, with a few clinging leaves still stubbornly hanging on. My breath made a cloud in front of my mouth. Maybe it was late October, early November? I shivered in my spring-appropriate clothes.

I turned the corner for my house. My sneakers beat a rhythm on the ground as I jogged up the front walk. I slowed to climb the steps.

I was home.

"Bee?" An incredulous voice behind me cried out.

Turning, I saw my old neighbor, Mrs. Teasley. She stood by her mailbox, her morning mail dangling in her hand. Her eyes widened as she saw my face.

"It's you," she gasped, dropping the mail. "Dear child, I thought, everyone thought—I mean, people supposed that you'd . . . well, never mind. It doesn't matter. You're here now. Are you all right?"

"I'm fine," I managed, doubling over and sucking in a breath. "I've been gone, I know, but—"

"We thought you were gone forever." She scooped up her letters and came to the fence that divided our lawns. Her eyes darted over me, like she was checking for bite marks. "It's good to see you, honey. You look well."

"I'm sorry I can't talk long," I said. "I need to speak to my father."

She raised both eyebrows. "But the whole family is gone to the city."

Her words hit me like a punch in the gut. The city?

"What?" I managed. My words came out in a squeak of disbelief.

Mrs. Teasley nodded. "Oh, honey. They left months ago. In the summer. Your stepmother is getting treatment there. You'd been gone so long, and your father said—"

I shook my head, cutting her off. "Thanks for telling me. I—I didn't know." I didn't want to know what lie he'd told her.

Her face crumpled with compassion. I looked at my feet. I needed to find Drew and Violet and everyone else.

"Mrs. Teasley?"

"Yes, dear?"

"Uh . . . what day is it? And, um, what month?"

Her wrinkled face didn't change expression at my odd, possibly deranged-sounding question, and I loved her for it. "Saturday, darling. And it's November now."

"Thanks." I stared down the stairs.

"Bee," she called after me.

I turned.

"Your mother was a good woman. Misunderstood, maybe, but a good woman. You look just like her. I always wanted to tell you that."

I smiled my thanks.

She went into her house, and I hit the road.

~

My stomach started twisting into a million knots as I got close to Drew's house. He lived only a few streets over from me, and I'd be there in a minute. All kinds of emotions filled my head and my heart. Had he forgotten about me? Would he slam the door in my face, frightened by rumors, or would he be happy to see me?

My feet slowed as I reached his front lawn.

Drawing a deep breath, I started up the front walk. I reached the front door and pressed the doorbell.

Footsteps thumped in the hall. I heard the sliding of the lock. I tried to compose my face. I didn't know if I should smile or look serious. I felt clammy and sick.

The door yanked open, and there he was.

"Hi," I tried, shyly.

"Hi." He was staring. "Bee?"

I kicked the ground with my shoe. "I know I've been gone a long time, but —"

He came out of his trance and grabbed me in a hug before I could say anything else. I froze in his arms, and then relaxed into him. A huge smile stretched across my face, and I hugged him back.

He was happy to see me!

Drew wanted to know everything. He ran inside and called Violet and the others to tell them to come over, then led me to the living room couch and made me sit. "Do you need anything? A drink, something to eat?"

"Maybe some water," I suggested. I was pretty thirsty from my run through the woods.

He nodded and disappeared into the kitchen. I looked around his living room. I'd only been in here once before. Dark curtains shut out the sunlight, and faded wallpaper gave the room an old, Victorian feel. Almost like the curse house.

My stomach lurched at the memory of it.

Drew came back with a glass of water. He sat next to me and watched me as I drained the glass. He keep staring at me like he was afraid I'd vanish in a poof of smoke.

"How have you been?" I said.

He laughed in disbelief, as if such a mundane question were unthinkable. He rubbed one hand through his hair and then reached for my hand. He stopped before touching me, though, and mumbled something.

"What was it like?" He asked after a long pause.

I shook my head. How could I talk about it? What could I possibly say that would sum up everything in a way he could understand? "Weird. Crazy. Nightmarish. Well, parts of it were almost nice, in a way, as weird as that sounds."

"Nice?"

"Some parts of it." I thought about Rose and Housekeeper and the origami roses and the pumpkin soup. Those parts had been nice.

"Are you okay?" He continued. "You aren't hurt or anything . . . ?"

"I'm fine." I smiled as wide as I could, hoping that would convince him.

"What's in your hand?"

I glanced down and saw I was still holding the key. It had turned back into paper, though, probably when I left the house.

"Oh. It's origami." I unfolded it. I'd used one of the pages from the book of letters. Scrawl covered the paper in dark strokes. My eye fell down the paragraphs as I spoke. "I made a key and used it to escape . . ."

The words jumped out at me. Marian's words. And my heart froze.

On the strands of our soul we hang the greatest of human virtues — bright gems that glitter in our hearts as we seek to polish them through use.

I scanned the rest of the paragraph, absorbing her words. My heart skipped a beat and then stumbled, beating faster. Sweat broke out across my palms. Was this the answer? Was this what she'd spoken of in the curse? We'd had it all wrong, hadn't we?

Then I thought of something else, something Marian had said to me the last time she'd seen me

Drew was still talking. I dragged my mind back to him. I could barely hear him above the roaring in my ears. His face wavered in my vision.

"...Still in shock. We thought you were never going to — well, we were worried. Your father said you were in the city, but we knew you'd never leave without saying goodbye. There were rumors, and I was so afraid that you weren't safe."

The words of the curse hummed in my brain, making it hard to listen. I licked my lips. "Drew —"

"I came to see you," he burst out. "I wanted to know for sure if you were there. I wanted to speak to you."

"I know," I said. "He told me later — yesterday, actually. I didn't know that you'd come. I'm so sorry I didn't get to see you —"

I heard Marian's voice, intruding in my head, drowning out my own voice. *"You do not understand the depth of guilt, do you? The agony of betrayal?"* I still couldn't believe that the curse had been so misleading. Nothing to do with necklaces at all.

"That's okay," Drew said, his voice cutting through my thoughts again. "It was good to know for sure where you were, at least. But I was pretty disappointed that I didn't get to see you. I would have gotten a kickin' grade on my journalism report if I could have cracked open the story that you were really at the curse house. There'd been so many rumors, you know . . ."

"Wait a second." I blinked, trying to swim through the swirl of emotions and thoughts to what he was saying. "You came to see me for a school project? Not to rescue me?"

He nodded, his smile freezing like he had just realized he'd said something wrong.

I struggled to speak normally. I was shaking. "I don't know what the rumors said, but I was trapped in the curse house and possibly in grave peril, and you didn't do anything about it? Didn't you think it was a bit odd that I just disappeared? You weren't even, you know, *worried* about me?"

Drew frowned. "Of course I was. We all were. But that guy said you were there of your own free will. You chose to go. It wasn't like you were forced or anything. You got to live in that swanky place while the rest of us were all worried about you. It was kind of selfish, actually. If you'd wanted to run away from your dad, you could have come to me or Violet or any of your other friends."

It was getting hard to breathe. I felt like I'd just run another mile, but at the same time my mind was clear. I'd been so stupid about him.

"I wasn't running away from anyone! I was a prisoner, Drew! Of course I was forced . . . I mean, I went of my own choice, to save my family because of my dad's dumb mistake, but then I didn't have a choice. You didn't even try to find your own girlfriend?"

"You're not my girlfriend," he said quickly. "Not anymore."

"I was at the time!"

Drew shifted. "I figured . . . I thought you wanted to break up, since you just ran off. I'm dating somebody else now."

"What?" I thought I was going to explode.

Drew was looking equally stunned. "So you didn't run away?"

"No, genius! And then we were working so hard to break that stupid curse—"

"We?"

"Will! The . . . the beast from the legends." Two thoughts hit me hard. First, how stupid that name sounded. Will wasn't a beast. He was just a guy, lonely and idealistic and stuck in a horrible place. Yeah, he was pig-headed and cranky and really stubborn sometimes, but he was also sweet and funny and generous and romantic.

Second, I didn't feel that sad about the news that Drew had moved on. Betrayed, yes. Enraged, yes. Hurt? Yeah. But sad?

Oddly, I was almost relieved. Here I had been feeling guilty because of my attraction to Will, and he hadn't even been worried about me!

I felt a stab of worry and concern about Will. He was my friend, and I cared about him. Deeply. And I'd abandoned him in probably the most crucial moment of his life.

He's my friend, and I care about him. That realization reverberated through my mind, freezing me in place and throwing every other feeling and thought into complete chaos. What was I doing? I'd left Will alone, with no way to break the curse without me, and barely any time. And now I knew the answer!

Sure, I was mad, but this was his *life* we were talking about. Mad could wait.

Suddenly I had a really, really bad feeling about this. How much time had been left in the hourglass? A few days? Weeks? Why did I suddenly feel as though I had no time at all?

"Look, I'm sorry about the breakup thing." Drew put his hand over mine. "Are you okay?"

"No, Drew. I'm not okay. Oh my goodness, you are an idiot. But I don't have time to even get into that now. I need to go. Because I've been a complete idiot too."

"But the others are coming over to see you! What's going on?"

"I'll see them later. I don't really have time to explain." I jumped up. Where was my stuff? Had I brought stuff? I grabbed my backpack off the floor. "Do you have a bike I can borrow?"

"Uhhh, sure." He stood too, looking like he wanted to argue. But he didn't. "It's in the garage."

I ran for the door.

"Wait, Bee! Where are you going?" Drew followed me into the garage.

"Back to the curse house! There's something I need to do!"

"Are you crazy? Why are you going back there? I thought you just said you'd been a prisoner!"

"Maybe I am crazy." I grabbed his bike and threw one leg over. "Tell everyone I love them and that I hope to see them soon, okay?"

"Bee! Wait!"

I didn't stop to respond.

I had to get back to Will before something terrible happened.

~

I reached the curse house much faster on the bike. When the faded stone and crumbling columns swung into sight, I let out a sigh of relief. I jumped down from the bike and let it fall. I ran across the leaf-strewn lawn and up the steps to the door.

The knob turned easily under my hand, just as it had the first day I'd entered the house. I rushed inside, my footsteps echoing loudly.

"Hello? Will? Rose?"

The house was still and etched with shadows. Nothing stirred in the crystal silence that confronted me. I hadn't realized how much the walls breathed, how much every corner and shadow and crack had been stuffed with strange, slithering magic until it was gone.

Now the walls were like bones, the rooms like empty, airless lungs.

I ran to the first door and wrenched it open, praying for the library, or Will's study, or any other place he might be. Instead I found a dusty music parlor. I shut the door and opened it again, trying for something else.

But it was just the same room again. A few dust motes drifted in the air, stirred up by my frantic slamming and opening.

What was happening? Had the curse been lifted? I sucked in a breath, trying to think. Why did I have such a terrible feeling in the pit of my stomach? Why did the house feel more like a corpse than anything else?

And most importantly, where was Will?

I went to the next door and found a hall. I took it. It was weird to be opening and closing doors normally again, instead of playing Russian roulette with them.

I came to the ballroom, massive and filled with smothering shadows. "Will? Housekeeper? Anyone?" The only answer was the echo of my own voice. I ran on. The next room was a parlor, with faded blue wallpaper decorated with roses and scrolls. Like Housekeeper's skin. I got a good look around, but didn't see anyone there either. I started to move on when something on the wall caught my eye and made me pause.

Was it just a shadow? I stepped closer, and my heartbeat stumbled. A water stain covered the wall beside the window. It almost looked like a person—there was the head, the shoulders, the arms . . .

"Housekeeper?" I whispered, stricken. Had she just melted into the wall? "Housekeeper!"

I heard no response. I stood there another moment, my mouth drying up and my heart hammering, and then I started running.

"Will? Rose?"

I had to find Will. I had to find them all.

His study was empty too. The hourglass lay in the middle of the room, shattered, the sand scattered across the rug in an S-shaped drift. It was no longer glowing.

"Will!" I shrieked, dropping to my knees. I scooped up handfuls of sand and tried to pour them back in the hourglass. What had he done? What had happened?

The mirror. Maybe he'd gone through it, maybe they'd all gone through—I whirled to look at it. My own face, drained of all color, gazed back at me like a startled animal.

I didn't want to go there alone again, but what else could I do?

On the floor I saw the book of letters. He'd been reading it here probably. Had he discovered an answer to the curse? Or had he given up because I'd left? Grabbing the book, I tucked it under my arm and took a deep breath.

Then I stepped through the mirror and into the Fey Lands.

SEVENTEEN

THE COOL RUSH of magic swept over my skin like a curtain of water. I held my breath, and the flashes of fire and ice rippled harmlessly over my skin. My head tingled, and then the world materialized around me in a burst of noise and color. Someone shouldered into me, pushing me forward. Another person pushed me back as they shoved past.

It took me a second to get my bearings. I was in the market place.

Clutching the book of letters to my chest, I scurried out of the stream of pedestrians and into a makeshift alley between two tents selling magic wares. An old elf woman leered at me.

"Want to sell your voice, Pretty One? I'll give you a good price for it!"

Will probably hated me right now, if he was even still alive. I wasn't sure what Marian was planning to do with him, if he was here. I needed to find them quickly.

"Um, no thanks," I said. "But you wouldn't happen to know where Marian the Witch is right now, would you?" I had this sinking feeling that if I found Marian, I'd find Will.

She shook her head vigorously. I fumbled with my clothes for something to offer as a bribe. Jewelry? Nope. A memory? Definitely not.

The book of letters! I tore out a sheet of paper and folded a rose. The old woman watched with amazement as it transformed in the palm of my hand.

"Amazing," she whispered. She reached out her hand, but I pulled the rose away.

"Where's Marian?"

"In the Hall of Roses," she said, her eyes still on the rose. "But you didn't hear it from me."

"Got it." I was already moving.

As I ran, I tried to formulate some kind of plan. What if I got there and Will was already permanently cursed, or worse, dead? What if Marian couldn't be talked down? Could I fight her? What would that entail?

I had this sneaking suspicion that a fight with her wouldn't involve hair-pulling and face-slapping.

Call me crazy.

I tore a few more pages from the book and shoved the rest into my backpack. I needed my hands free. I stuffed the loose pages in my belt. A very hazy plan was started to take shape in my head. It was probably suicidal.

With that cheerful thought ringing in my mind, I headed straight for the ballroom.

~

A crowd had gathered. Humans, faeries, trolls, and

other magical creatures milled around or stood transfixed by what was happening. But nobody was doing anything to help. I pushed my way into the fray, not caring who I jostled. I could hear Marian's voice.

"Are you ready for a life of unending agony, William? Are you ready to be a beast forever?"

Relief rushed through me. It hadn't happened yet. She was probably playing cat and mouse with him, which was horrible, but it gave me time.

I reached the edge of the crowd and stopped short. Marian stood in the center of the room, her hands on her hips. Will was on the floor in front of her, crumpled in a heap. His face was buried in his arm, and all I could see was his tangle of dark hair and one of his hands, outstretched as if he'd been pleading with her.

"Your Curse Girl left you," Marian said. "You've failed the test. Your time is up."

Will's voice was muffled. "Please, just spare my sister. And the servants . . . they've done nothing to you."

"Silence," Marian hissed. "You're all alone now. It's time."

I finished what I was folding. I spoke loud so my voice would carry over the murmur of the crowd.

"You're wrong, Marian. He's not alone."

The witch swung around. Will's head snapped up, and his eyes found mine. A happy rush poured through me when our eyes met.

I was so glad to see him.

"You came back," he said, and he sounded like a little kid. Lost, sad, and happy, all at once.

I took a step towards him. "I was stupid to leave you like that. I shouldn't have done it, and I won't do it again."

Will shook his head weakly. Blood dripped down his forehead and onto his cheek. "No, Bee — you should get out of here now before — "

"It doesn't matter," Marian interrupted. She gave me a poisonous smile. "You still haven't broken the curse. You don't know how."

"Now that's where you're wrong," I said.

Marian's smile sharpened.

I gulped a breath and kept talking. ""We found your book of letters. I read one of them this morning, actually. And I realized something." I took another step towards Will. "What were the words of the curse? *Unless the Brightest Pearl He Grasps.* Naturally, we thought this meant an actual pearl."

Marian's eyes narrowed.

"You see," I continued. "We were looking for stupid necklaces. We didn't realize you were using a metaphor at first. Deliberately confusing, I might add. Anyway, I read your letter. I made it into a key and when I got back outside I could see it without magic, and I saw what you wrote to Robert. You told him that all the gifts of love, all the human virtues are like bright pearls on a necklace, but the brightest pearl of all is the gift of forgiveness when the one you love has wronged you."

"At first I thought you meant that you had to forgive Robert for what he'd done to you, but then I remembered something you said to me. You asked me if I knew the depth of guilt, or the agony of betrayal? I don't think it was Robert who betrayed you."

She was absolutely still, waiting for me to finish. Her fingers curled into a fist.

"I think it was you who betrayed Robert."

Will sucked in a sharp breath. Marian was silent.

"The baby," I said. "Robert leaving you . . . it all points to one thing, doesn't it?"

Marian shivered.

"And I guess you thought it was pretty clever of you to make him forgive you — for real — before you'd lift the werewolf curse on him. Of course, Will doesn't love you, so when you cursed him by mistake, the solution was completely out of your hands, whether you wanted to release him from it or not. And as the curse consumed him, it consumed you too. It made you crazy."

Her mouth opened and closed, like her words were stuck in her throat. She didn't try to deny anything I'd said.

I turned to Will. He was raised up on one arm, staring at me with a mixture of admiration, amazement, and terror.

"Will, do you love me?" It was a very abrupt question, and he was taken off guard. I waved a hand. "Not in a, you know, romantic way or anything, but — "

"Yes," he said, cutting me off before I rambled further. "I really do. I've never thought higher of anyone else before in my life."

"Do you forgive me for running off and leaving you in the lurch?"

"Of course," he said.

Now it was my turn. I felt as if I were proposing. "Will, I think you're infuriating, frustrating, and thoroughly conceited sometimes."

His expression faltered, and he swallowed hard. He nodded.

"But," I added, my voice softening, "You're also one of the coolest guys I've ever met, and for whatever reason, I care about you. A lot. I daresay you could call it love. Yeah. Love."

I looked at the crowd, which had fallen silent.

"He was pretty mean to me in the beginning, and then after I started to fall for him he lied to me about some things. He really upset me and hurt me. But you know what? When you love somebody, you give them another chance. Because that's what love is. A lifetime of second chances."

Will's face had softened. Our gazes connected, and I swear I felt the electricity jump across the room from his body to mine. "I'm sorry I lied," he said. "It was so wrong of me. Forgive me?"

"Yes," I said. "I forgive you, Will."

A sharp, electric tingle ran over my skin like a shock from a light socket. Will's head snapped back, and he fall backwards on the ground with a cry of pain.

A gust of wind roared through the room, blowing my hair back. Marian's eyes fluttered, and her skin shriveled like an apple left out in the sun. When the wind stilled, she looked old and withered. She caught sight of her hands and gasped, horrified.

"Will?" I called. He wasn't moving. I started towards him, but the witch blocked my way.

"Not so fast," she snarled. "You may have broken the curse, but I'm not just going to let you walk away."

"We broke the curse! You have to let us go. Isn't that in the rules or something?"

Her lips curled in a sneer. "There are no rules, little girl."

"Beauty, watch out!"

Marian raised both hands over her head. Something hit me hard, knocking me sideways. I skidded across the floor. When I looked up, Storm was doubled over in the middle of the room, glaring at the witch.

"She broke the curse. You're being dishonorable."

"Out of my way, elf," Marian snapped. With a flick of her fingers, she tossed him aside like a rag doll.

I scrambled up to my feet. Marian stalked towards me like a lion approaching its prey.

"Apparently you've made some friends," she said. "But they won't help you."

Will struggled to his feet. "Marian," he shouted. "Leave her alone."

Marian stopped. She crooked her finger at me, and I fell to my knees.

"No!" Will lunged, and Marian threw him back with her magic. He hit the wall and slid to the floor with a groan. Blood bubbled between his teeth.

Marian turned back to me.

"Now then," she purred. "There's no one else left to shield you from your fate. I'm going to turn you into dust." She wiggled her fingers, and a shimmering blue light appeared between her palms.

A thought clicked in my head. Shield. *Shield!*

"Beauty!" Will yelled again, but I was way ahead of him. I knew exactly what to do now.

I grabbed a sheet of paper from my belt and began folding.

Marian hurled the magic at me. I threw up my hands, and the object in them turned real at the last possible moment. The magic hit the mirror and flew back into Marian's shocked face. She froze in a single, crackling moment, her expression preserved forever in horrified shock.

And then she dissolved into a pile of dust.

I collapsed on the ground with a sob of relief.

It was over.

This nightmare was finally finished.

The witch was dead.

Will crawled to my side and pulled me to him in a careful hug. Was it my imagination, or did I catch a glimpse of the faery called Anna giving me a thumbs-up in the crowd?

"Are you okay?" I said, leaning back to study his face. The cut on his forehead had dried. He winced as I touched his side.

"Broken ribs, maybe. Otherwise just got the wind knocked out of me. You?"

"I'm fine." I looked around for Storm. He'd been honorable after all. He'd helped us. I spotted the night elf slipping through the door. He turned, and I raised my hand to beckon him back, but he just shook his head and winked.

I guessed he wanted to preserve his reputation.

"Where did you learn to do that bit with the mirror?" Will gasped, gazing at the place where Marian's dust lay in a pile.

"A faery." I wiped at my eyes with the back of my hand, and with the other I hugged him tight. I didn't want to let him go. I'd come so close to losing one of the best persons I'd ever met.

His eyes widened at the word *faery*, and he shook his head.

"You," he said, "Are amazing. Have I ever told you that?"

"Not enough," I said. I touched his face lightly.

"Are you sure you're okay?"

"Great," he said, wincing as he got to his feet. He pulled me up after him. "Do I look less . . . beastly?"

The magical blue quality of his eyes had faded, leaving them ordinary and blue-gray like a normal person's. His scar was still a soft, pearly white, but the otherworldly glint had faded. His black hair was rumpled from his fall. But he was beautiful.

"You've never looked better," I said. And I meant it.

EIGHTEEN

WHEN WILL AND I staggered through the mirror again, everyone was waiting for us. Rose bounded forward, grabbing me tight in a hug.

"You did it!" She squealed, squeezing my ribs.

Over her head, I saw the servants — Housekeeper, Butler, and the others. Housekeeper's face shone with a healthy peach glow. No more wallpaper skin. Butler had a pleasant smile and a balding head. He bowed to me gravely.

"Hannah," Housekeeper said to me, her grin splitting her face. "My name is Hannah! I remember!"

"Mine is Winifred," Rose said, wrinkling her nose. "I think I'll stick with my curse name, thank you very much."

She let go of me and ran to Will. I stared around us at the house. With the curse magic gone, everything looked old and faded. There were holes in the roof where the shingles had torn away. Sunlight streamed through them, making a shifting pattern on the floor. It was beautiful.

Will took my hand and kissed it. Together we began to walk through the ruined rooms. "What are we going to do now?"

I slipped my arm around his waist. My smile stretched wide as I realized the wealth of delights that waited for us. I never thought I'd get to show someone from the past around the present day.

"There are so many things you're going to need to do. Let me think . . . Ice cream. You definitely need to have some double-chocolate chunk ice cream. And a hamburger. Movies, we'll have to introduce you to that. And we'll need to find some place for you guys to live—oh, and my family went to the city! We need to find them. You and Rose can go with me. And the servants—they'll need somebody to help them adjust to modern society too."

"Your family?" His forehead wrinkled in concern. "How do you know?"

"I found that out when I left this morning. I found out a lot of things, actually. Like the fact that Drew isn't my boyfriend any more. He's dating someone else."

"What?" Will stopped walking. He looked thunderstruck. "Is he crazy?"

I waved a hand. I was totally over the whole being-dumped-without-knowing-it thing. "Believe me, I'm no catch. By the way, do you have any money left in this old mansion?"

"My father's inheritance should still be waiting for me," Will said, still frowning. His eyes searched mine like he was deciding whether or not to say something else.

"Good, because you probably need to get your GED and then go to college. You're probably going to have to get a job, you know. And Rose —"

"Beauty," he said.

"And you'll have to get your driver's license —"

"Beauty," he repeated.

I paused. "Yes, Will?"

"I told you before, you're the most beautiful girl I've ever seen. You're also the bravest, smartest, and kindest." His blue eyes shimmered as he looked at me. "And before we do any of these other things you have planned, there's something else I need to take care of first."

He stopped and took my hand in both of his.

"Bee, will you do me the incredible honor of becoming my girlfriend?"

My smile almost split my face.

"Absolutely."

And then I kissed him.

SPECIAL THANKS

I could never have made it this far without all the lovely, generous, amazing people in my life.

Scott, for providing support for each new project I start, for believing in me every step of the way, for reading every book I write, and for formatting my ebooks. I love you!

Nikki and Amy, for reading and giving enthusiastic praise and feedback. You guys are awesome.

Rebecca, for being an amazing critique partner. You're a superhero when it comes to editing, and I salute you.

Jaimie, for being my beta reader and partner in querying for all these months. You are awesome.

My family, for all your love and support!

ABOUT THE AUTHOR

Kate Avery Ellison lives in Georgia with her husband Scott and their two spoiled cats. When she isn't writing, she enjoys watching NBC comedy shows, playing strategy games, and eating ice cream cake. While it's true that she's currently writing a zombie novel, don't let that fool you. She is decidedly Team Unicorn.

Learn more about Kate Avery Ellison's upcoming books and other writing projects by visiting her online at http://thesouthernscrawl.blogspot.com/.

15534741R00103

Made in the USA
Lexington, KY
02 June 2012